P9-CNI-041

"We can't get caught up in this whole fake-engagement thing and lose sight of who we really are," Josie said.

"I haven't lost sight of anything. And I'm well aware of who we are...and what I want."

Why did that sound so menacing in the most delicious of ways? Why was her body tingling so much from such simple touches when she'd firmly told herself to not get carried away?

Wait. Was he leaning in closer?

"Reese, what are you doing?" she whispered.

"Testing a theory."

His mouth grazed hers like a feather. Her knees literally weakened as she leaned against him for support. Reese continued to hold her hand against his chest, but he wrapped the other arm around her waist, urging her closer.

There was no denying the sizzle or spark or whatever the hell was vibrating between them.

* * *

Scandalous Engagement by Jules Bennett is part of the Lockwood Lightning series.

Dear Reader,

Welcome to the final installment of Lockwood Lightning! I hope you've enjoyed the journey so far because Reese and Josie are about to explode onto the scene!

I admit I'm a sucker for a good friends-to-lovers trope. I had such fun with this opening, and Reese is probably one of my favorite heroes. He's fun, laid-back, but oh-so-sexy and demanding. Josie is quite a match for him, though. She's definitely a force, which is just what Reese needs.

Oh, did I mention they're faking an engagement? Another one of my favorite ways to torture my characters.

I do hope you love *Scandalous Engagement* as much as I loved writing it. Lockwood Lightning has been in my mind for quite some time now and I'm thrilled to have this complete series out into the world.

Happy reading!

Jules

JULES BENNETT

———

SCANDALOUS ENGAGEMENT

If you purchased this book without a cover you should be aware
that this book is stolen property. It was reported as "unsold and
destroyed" to the publisher, and neither the author nor the
publisher has received any payment for this "stripped book."

Recycling programs
for this product may
not exist in your area.

ISBN-13: 978-1-335-20917-7

Scandalous Engagement

Copyright © 2020 by Jules Bennett

All rights reserved. No part of this book may be used or reproduced in any
manner whatsoever without written permission except in the case of brief
quotations embodied in critical articles and reviews.

This is a work of fiction. Names, characters, places and incidents
are either the product of the author's imagination or are used fictitiously.
Any resemblance to actual persons, living or dead, businesses,
companies, events or locales is entirely coincidental.

This edition published by arrangement with Harlequin Books S.A.

For questions and comments about the quality of this book,
please contact us at CustomerService@Harlequin.com.

Harlequin Enterprises ULC
22 Adelaide St. West, 40th Floor
Toronto, Ontario M5H 4E3, Canada
www.Harlequin.com

Printed in U.S.A.

USA TODAY bestselling author **Jules Bennett** has published over sixty books and never tires of writing happy endings. Writing strong heroines and alpha heroes is Jules's favorite way to spend her workdays. Jules hosts weekly contests on her Facebook fan page and loves chatting with readers on Twitter, Facebook and via email through her website. Stay up-to-date by signing up for her newsletter at julesbennett.com.

Books by Jules Bennett

Harlequin Desire

The Rancher's Heirs

Twin Secrets
Claimed by the Rancher
Taming the Texan
A Texan for Christmas

Two Brothers

Montana Seduction
California Secrets

Lockwood Lightning

An Unexpected Scandal
Scandalous Engagement

Visit her Author Profile page at Harlequin.com, or julesbennett.com, for more titles.

You can also find Jules Bennett on Facebook, along with other Harlequin Desire authors, at Facebook.com/harlequindesireauthors!

To my very best friend, Michael.
Thank you for giving me
the best happily-ever-after.

One

Josie Coleman flung open the front door of her beachfront home and rolled her eyes.

"I've told you for years to just come on in," she exclaimed as she stepped back. "Why do you insist on knocking?"

Her best friend, Reese Conrad, shrugged like he always did when he refused to just walk into her home, where he was always welcome. She always just walked right into *his* house when she stopped by. They didn't live far from each other on this stretch of beach in Sandpiper Cove, North Carolina. It was one of the things she treasured about the place.

"Respect," he replied in that low, gravelly tone of his.

She always asked the same question and he always gave the same one-word response. She'd also offered him a key, but he always said he didn't need one because he only stopped by when she was home.

Typically, they were either at his place, out on his yacht or traveling together when their schedules permitted.

"I thought you were out of town on a work trip." Josie walked through the spacious open layout of her living room and headed back toward the wall of open glass doors leading to her patio. "I'm having coffee if you want to join me."

"It's five o'clock in the evening."

She stopped and threw a glance over her shoulder. "What does that have to do with the love of coffee?"

He laughed and shook his head. Like he didn't know her mad love of coffee?

"I'm good," he replied as he followed her out onto the outdoor living area. "And I cut my trip short because I had seen all I needed to see."

Something crossed through his eyes, something almost…sad. Reese was usually the happiest guy she knew. He had everything—a successful career in the restaurant industry, parents who doted on him and loved him unconditionally, her as a best friend. What more could he need?

Yet something was off.

"Everything all right?" Josie asked as she settled into her lounger and curled her hands around her favorite coffee mug, the one Reese had given her last Christmas.

Reese shoved his hands in his pockets and glanced out at the horizon. It was impossible to be in a bad mood with this view, but she couldn't get a bead on what was going through his head. That was a first. They always knew each other's thoughts. They could be at a party or in a crowded room and one look at each other and they'd smile or nod, knowing exactly what the other had on their mind.

There was something to be said for the unique bond between lifelong besties.

"Honestly—"

Her shrill ringtone cut off anything he was about to admit. Josie sat her mug back on the glass table and picked up her cell, then muttered a string of curses.

"What now?" she answered, totally not in the mood for her ex-husband.

Out of the corner of her eye, she caught Reese staring at her. Reese knew the mess she'd gotten into by marrying the wrong guy on a whim. The marriage had been a mistake and she was still trying to figure out how she'd temporarily lost her mind and agreed to marry a man she didn't love.

Oh, Chris was a nice guy; he just wasn't for her,

and lately he'd been trying to win her back. There was no going back.

"Listen, I'm not trying to be rude," she said now into the phone, "but it's not going to happen. We're divorced for a reason." She sat up and swung her legs to the side. "You're a great guy, but we're just not good together, Chris."

Yet he'd been calling and texting more and more. Josie could see where Chris would be confused. They'd only dated for three months before they'd up and eloped. Never in her life had she made rash choices—she prided herself on being just as regimented and predictable as her military father—yet she'd been spontaneous with one of the most important decisions of her life.

For someone normally so methodical about her life, that rush to the courthouse had been completely out of character. But Reese had just gotten engaged and that act had made her wonder if *she* should be entering the next chapter in her life as well.

Obviously, the answer had been no.

Now here they were: she was divorced and Reese had a broken engagement. Maybe they just needed to stay as they were, as they had been for years. They were happy hanging out and traveling together. Having significant others enter the mix would only mess up their perfect best-friend vibe.

But she had yet to get Chris to understand her point of view. Unfortunately, no matter how much she told him she wasn't getting back together with him, he didn't get it. Maybe if he believed there was someone else he would realize there was absolutely no room for him in her life.

"I've moved on," she blurted into the phone as she came to her feet. Josie darted her gaze to Reese, who merely raised his brows in surprise. "That's right. He's here right now, so I have to go."

Josie disconnected the call and tossed her cell onto the lounger she'd just vacated. Reese continued to stare at her, but she just sighed and shrugged.

"He's getting relentless," she defended. "I had to say something."

"So I'm your rebound guy?"

Josie smiled, feeling a tiny bit guilty for using Reese. "He doesn't know who's here, and it was the first thing that came into my head. He has to think I've moved on with someone else or he'll keep wasting his time trying to win me back. He has to let it go."

She crossed the patio and placed her hand on his arm. "I'm sorry I used you as the scapegoat. Let's forget about Chris. What were you getting ready to say before?" she asked.

"I went to Green Valley, Tennessee," he told her. "It wasn't just about business."

Josie dropped her arm and wiggled her brows. "Something personal? A woman?"

He hadn't dated since he'd ended things with his

fiancée nearly a year ago. He'd been too busy taking over his family's posh restaurant empire, with establishments up and down the East Coast. Recently his father had suffered a heart attack, which led to open-heart surgery. Reese's parents were now at some tropical resort to celebrate his life and their new retirement.

So what had Reese been doing in Tennessee if the trip didn't pertain to his business?

Before he could explain further, the doorbell chimed and echoed through the house and out the patio doors. Why did she have to keep getting interrupted when she was just trying to get the scoop on her friend, who obviously had something serious going on?

"Sorry about that," she told him as she came to her feet. "I'm not expecting anyone, so just give me one second."

Josie crossed the living area to the foyer and glanced through the sidelight. Seriously? What would it take for Chris to get the hint?

On a frustrated sigh, Josie opened the door. Her ex stood before her. The man was tall and strong, and always took pride in his athletic build. He wasn't unattractive. He just wasn't the right guy for her. If she could keep him in the friend zone, that would be fine, but he didn't want to accept that.

"Chris," Josie groaned. "We just hung up."

"I know, I know, but I had just pulled up to your

house when I called and I only want a few minutes of your time."

Chris stared at Josie with his heart in his eyes and she wanted to tell him to go out with some dignity, for pity's sake.

"I only wanted five minutes in person," Chris explained. "That's all. Just five minutes."

"Chris, we're not doing this again. We're not meant for each other."

"But what if we are?"

Before she could respond, Reese's arm slid around her waist and he pulled her against his side.

"Everything all right, babe?"

Babe? What the hell was he doing?

She glanced from Reese to Chris and remembered what she'd said earlier. Well, damn. Looked like she'd caused a minor mess here.

Chris's eyes went from Josie, to Reese, and back again.

"Can we talk alone?" he implored.

"Say what you want," Reese stated with a smile. "My fiancée doesn't keep secrets from me. Right, lover?"

Was he out of his ever-loving mind? She didn't need his help, and he was making this uncomfortable situation an impossible one.

Engaged? That was taking things a bit far. She'd only mentioned that she'd moved on, not that she'd moved on and was ready to walk down the aisle again.

"You're marrying this guy?" Chris asked. "I always knew there was something more than friends going on with you two. Were you seeing him the entire time we were together?"

"What? No, of course not," she said defensively, wondering how she could circle around and restart this conversation with less chaos and confusion.

"As you can see, Josie is not available," Reese added with another squeeze of her hip. "We're getting ready to go out for the evening."

His hand dipped down over the curve of her hip and too many thoughts and emotions hit her at once. First, why was he being so handsy? Second, was she *enjoying* this?

She shouldn't have a rush of tingles from her best friend's touch. It wasn't like they'd never touched before.

But they'd never touched like this. Not in a faux intimate way.

And it was like something shifted between them.

He was so firm, so strong, and he smelled too damn good.

No.

She shouldn't be thinking of Reese's muscle tone and his cologne. That would only lead to trouble, right?

Yes, trouble with a big fat capital *T.*

The last time she'd let herself step outside her comfort zone, she'd found herself married to the wrong man.

Reese was her *friend*.

Her best friend.

And she needed to keep him in that zone. She liked her life nice and tidy. She liked having everything, and everyone, in their own place.

But that excellent muscle tone...

To save her sanity, Josie extracted herself from Reese and offered Chris a sympathetic smile.

"I do hope you can move on," she told him. "There's a woman out there for you. She's just not me."

Chris's expression went from disbelief, to anger, to...hell, she wasn't sure, but the man wasn't happy.

His eyes scrutinized her. "Are you sure this is what you want? I mean, you're not even wearing a ring. You deserve better. You know I treated you like a queen."

Before Josie could reply, Reese stepped forward.

"What she deserves and doesn't deserve is none of your concern anymore. You've had more than that five minutes you asked for."

Without another word, Reese stepped aside and slammed the door in Chris's face. Josie stared at the space that had just been open and couldn't believe Reese had the audacity to...to...

"Are you serious?" she exclaimed.

Reese turned and started back toward her patio as if he hadn't just acted like a complete jerk. She marched right after him. This was her house, her ex, and Reese wasn't just going to do whatever he wanted and manipulate the situation to his liking!

"Are you going to explain yourself?" she demanded as she stepped outside.

Reese shrugged and took a seat on the sofa. "Explain what? He called and you told him you were in a relationship, so when he showed up, obviously I'm the one who had to play the role."

Josie tucked her hair behind her ears and crossed her arms over her chest. In the last twenty minutes, her ex-husband had said he truly believed they could get back together and her best friend had claimed to be her fiancé. Even stalling for a few seconds trying to gather her thoughts didn't calm her mood or give her any more clarity…especially over the fact that she'd liked Reese's touch more than she should.

"Engaged seems a little over-the-top, don't you think?" she asked.

"Not really. The guy is persistent. You have to push back with people like that. Subtlety isn't something they understand."

"Oh, an engagement and slamming the door in his face were far from subtle hints."

He offered her a wink and a grin. "You're welcome."

Josie growled and clenched her fists. Reese might

be her very best friend, but he could be quite infuriating at times…in an adorable kind of way. He meant well, but sometimes that alpha quality took over and common sense vanished.

"Better drink your coffee before it gets cold," he added, pointing to her forgotten mug.

Josie reached for the drink and crossed to where he sat with that smug smirk on his face.

"I really want to throw this in your face," she grumbled.

"Aw, darling. Is that anyway to treat your new fiancé? Be nice or I won't get you that ring you need."

"You know he's going to tell people what just happened," she informed him. "We're both in the public eye. How will we dodge this?"

If she had a job where people didn't recognize her or didn't know her name, Reese's engagement claim wouldn't be a big deal. But considering Reese was a billionaire mogul splashed all over the internet right now for taking over his family's empire, and she was an influencer and columnist for the country's top-selling magazine, there was no way an engagement between them would go unnoticed.

"I'm not too worried about the public." Reese shrugged. Again with that damn shrug, like this was no big deal. "Just wait and see how it plays out. He may surprise you by keeping quiet, or we may need to play it up. What kind of stone would you like in your ring?"

Josie narrowed her eyes. "I'm going to need to switch to wine for this conversation."

Ignoring his chuckle, she stepped back into her house and moved into the kitchen. From her vantage point at the wine fridge, Josie stared out at Reese, who didn't seem to mind that he'd just upended both of their lives. He simply sat in one of the sturdy wicker chairs and stared out at the horizon.

When he'd first arrived today, he'd said he needed to talk. All she'd managed to learn was that he'd been away on personal business. If it hadn't concerned a woman, then what else would it be? He didn't have much of a social life. If he went out to dinners, they were all work-related, and the majority of the time, those dinners were in his own restaurant.

The man worked like a maniac, and that was saying something coming from *Cocktails & Classy*'s most celebrated columnist. Josie never took a day off either, but at least she could work from home and only travel to the headquarters in Atlanta when she absolutely had to. Reese traveled all over, constantly on the lookout for new ways to keep his restaurants fresh and upscale.

She poured a glass of pinot and swirled the contents before heading back out. She never got tired of the ocean breeze, and she always slid open the wall of glass doors when she was home. The added outdoor living space was what had sold her on this house right after her divorce.

Now that she'd calmed down a little, Josie stepped around the coffee table and took a seat on the sofa across from Reese.

"Want to tell me why you got so territorial?" she asked.

He propped his feet on the coffee table and laced his fingers behind his head as he stared at her, since she now blocked his line of sight to the ocean.

"Besides the fact that he was the wrong man for you to marry in the first place? I was trying to help you out."

Josie took a sip and set her glass on the table before leaning forward and keeping her gaze locked on his. "I can fight my own battles."

"You shouldn't have to," he retorted.

While she appreciated the way he was always ready to protect her, she didn't need him to. His failed engagement and her failed marriage had really opened her eyes to the fact that there was no rush to move on to what was expected. Who said she had to get married right now? There was no magical age when she had to be married, and who said she had to be married at all?

But she knew Reese might want a family and a married life of his own.

The day would come when he would find the woman he wanted to spend his life with.

The thought unsettled her. Or maybe it was that Josie could still feel his fingertips along her waist and her hip. She shouldn't still be tingling in those spots, but she was—which was both confusing and frustrating.

Josie's cell buzzed on the table and she glanced to the screen at the same time Reese muttered a curse. Chris's name popped up with an unread message.

"He's still not taking the hint?" Reese asked. "I slammed the door in his face."

She didn't bother opening the text; she would deal with it later…or not.

"Maybe I should've just talked to him for a bit," she stated.

"No. Every time you talk to him, that gives him hope. You just need to cut all ties."

Reese was right, but she really hated being rude. She'd told Chris as nicely as possible that they were really over, and they'd been divorced for six months already. Wasn't that enough of a sign that she was moving on? One would think divorce would be enough "cutting ties," but Chris hadn't wanted the divorce to begin with.

"Don't worry," Reese added. "He'll get the hint once he sees us together and notices my car out front when he drives by."

Josie laughed. "It's not like you'll be here twenty-four hours a day, Reese."

His eyes flashed to hers. "Sure I will. I can work from here. It will be tricky, and I have to do some traveling still, but you're the top priority in my life right now. So which bedroom do you want me to take?"

"Bedroom?" she asked. "You mean—"

A naughty grin spread across his face that sent a curl of unwanted arousal through her.

This was her best friend…what was going on?

"I'm moving in, honey."

Two

Well, this wasn't what he'd planned when he'd arrived at Josie's house yesterday. But damn if he hadn't gotten completely sidetracked by feeling her against his side, having that curvy hip beneath his hand.

He'd always known his best friend was sexy as hell, but she'd always been his friend. Now she was his fake fiancée…how the hell was he supposed to play this out?

What had he gotten them into?

Yesterday he'd needed her advice; he'd needed her guidance and her shoulder to lean on. Not that he did that often, but his life had imploded and he had nowhere else to go.

He was still trying to process everything himself. From receiving a cryptic letter at his office while his father was recovering from heart surgery, to finding out his father wasn't his father at all...if the letter from a deceased woman was actually true.

Reese sank down on the edge of the bed in the guest bedroom of Josie's home and clutched the letter in his hands. When he'd left for Tennessee several days ago, he'd told Josie he'd be gone a week. He'd come back after two days.

Traveling from Green Valley, Tennessee, back to Sandpiper Cove, North Carolina, had only been an hour's flight. Those were the perks of owning your own plane and being your own pilot. He'd taken the time going both ways to think about all that had happened...he still didn't have a clear picture or any answers.

He'd gone to Hawkins Distillery a few days ago and met with Sam Hawkins and Nick Campbell, the two men who were supposedly Reese's half brothers. Nick's late mother had apparently wanted to leave behind a deathbed confession by distributing letters for the three men about their true paternity. She was the one who had mailed the letter to Reese.

They all shared the same father—Rusty Lockwood, billionaire mogul of Lockwood Lightning. Everyone knew the world-renowned moonshine company, but not many knew the man behind it... including Reese.

A week ago, he'd hired an investigator to dig up everything that wasn't easily accessible to the public, and Reese had also been doing his own online research. On paper, or the internet as the case may be, Rusty appeared to be a saint. The man owned the largest moonshine distillery in the world and donated thousands of dollars each year to Milestones, a charity for children with disabilities.

Unfortunately, last week, Rusty had been arrested for skimming from that same charity, and according to Sam and Nick, Rusty was the devil himself. Both guys had dealt with Rusty for years and neither one had a kind thing to say. They weren't happy with the knowledge that Rusty was their biological father.

Reese didn't know what to believe, because all of this had blown up in his face so fast and come without warning. He didn't like being blindsided by anything, especially not a revelation that meant he might have been betrayed and lied to his entire life.

The letter had arrived while his father was in the hospital, but once he was released, he and Reese's mom had gone on a relaxing vacation with the doctor's blessing and Reese didn't want to mess up their time away.

There had just been so much all at once... His father's health, the shifting responsibilities of the business, the letter claiming Reese wasn't his parents' child...

But by the time his parents got back home, Reese

hoped he would have a solid plan and some much-needed answers.

Should Reese confront them? Or did he just let this knowledge go and ignore the past? What was the actual truth in all of this? There were so many questions and part of him wished he'd never learned the truth, but the other part of him wanted to know the history...*his* history.

Reese refolded the letter and sat it on the night-stand before coming to his feet. He hadn't gotten much sleep last night, mostly because this wasn't his home and he wasn't used to that cushy bed with all the pillows.

Josie might be very strict and straitlaced when it came to her fashion sense and her career, but she did love a cozy-feeling home. Granted, everything in her house was either white or gray. She really did lack color in her life, but he wouldn't change her for anything.

Especially those damn curves.

Who had known how well she'd fit intimately against his side? Just that simple gesture had con-jured up a night of fantasies he shouldn't have al-lowed himself when it came to his best friend. Didn't he have enough going on in his life without adding an unwanted sexual attraction to Josie?

Reese rubbed a hand over his bare chest and pad-ded from the room and down the hallway toward the kitchen. He needed coffee, because this was the time of day when it was actually acceptable to have a cup. It was too damn early, but he might as well get his day started.

He'd visited here so many times over the years, but he'd never made coffee, so he searched through her cabinets, trying to be quiet because he was positive she was still asleep. He hadn't heard a word from her this morning, and he also knew she wasn't an early riser.

He, on the other hand, had too much to do, including following up with his assistant about the RSVP to the new restaurant opening in Manhattan in two weeks.

Conrad's was moving up the East Coast and opening a big new space in New York. Reese couldn't wait to get into his favorite city. Manhattan had always been a goal of his.

He'd grown up here in Sandpiper Cove and he absolutely loved the beach. Loved it so much, he'd purchased his own private beach with his home, which was not far from Josie. His yacht was docked at the end of his own pier and he didn't want to lay his head down anywhere else.

But this new restaurant in Manhattan would be all his. He'd inherited his father's string of upscale restaurants from Miami up to Boston, but this was his first venture on his own and he had a few changes in place that he was excited to test.

"Good heavens."

Reese turned from the coffeepot to find Josie standing in the doorway, her hand over her chest, her eyes fixed on his. But his eyes immediately locked on the tiny shorts and tank she wore. The outfit left little to the imagination…and last night he'd done plenty of imagining.

"Could you put some clothes on?" she grumbled as she shuffled in.

Reese couldn't help but grin as she made her way to the cabinet and pulled down a mug. Her hair was all in disarray, like she'd had a fight with her pillow all night, and those pj's, black of course, weren't covering much, either. The simple tank dipped too low and the shorts literally covered the essentials and nothing more.

His body stirred in response.

There were some things he could control, like not telling her he'd like to strip her down and pleasure her beyond anything she'd ever known. But there were other things, like his arousal, that weren't quite so easy to hide.

Damn it. He had to get a grip. This was Josie. He couldn't risk a quick romp just because suddenly his hormones had woken up and realized she was sexier than he'd known.

They were friends…nothing more.

"You've seen me in swim trunks. This is hardly any different," he replied, taking the mug from her hands. "Go sit. I'll get this for you."

She shoved the hair from her face and went to the bench at her kitchen table. "Trunks are one thing, but boxer briefs are another. If you're staying here, put some damn pants on."

Reese poured two cups of coffee, leaving hers black to match her wardrobe and her bleak mood.

"I don't recall you being this grouchy in the mornings," he told her as he sat across from her. "I know you're more of a night owl, but this is a new side."

She curled her hands around her mug. "This is my only side before caffeine. Be quiet so I can enjoy it."

Reese sipped his hot coffee and waited on Little Miss Sunshine to perk up. Clearly, she'd had a restless night, too. He didn't even try to hide the fact that he was staring at her. She looked like a hot mess, which irritated the hell out of him because his boxer briefs were becoming more and more snug. There was going to be no hiding anything in a few minutes.

"Shouldn't you be lifting weights or jogging or going to some meeting where you fire people?" she asked around her mug.

Reese laughed. "Glad to know what you think of a day in the life of Reese Conrad."

She merely shrugged, causing one slinky shoulder strap to slip down her arm. Reese's eyes landed on that black string and he barely resisted reaching out to adjust it.

Hands to yourself.

A physical relationship would certainly change

things between them, but the main question was—
would they be better or worse?

Wait. What?

Why was he even letting his mind travel to that
space? He needed to get control over his wayward
thoughts and keep himself in check.

"You don't have to stay here, you know."

His focus shifted back to her face. She stared at
him over the rim of her mug. Those dark eyes never
let on to what she was truly thinking…just another
way they were so alike. Both held their emotions
close to their chest.

"How many times did Chris text you last night?"
he asked.

Josie's eyes darted away as she mumbled something under her breath. He thought he heard a stag-
gering number, but even one was one too many at
this point. Beyond the fact that they were divorced,
she'd blatantly told Chris no and Reese had mentioned they were engaged. A lie, sure, but Chris
didn't know that. The man should back off.

"All the more reason for me to stay for a while,"
Reese replied.

Maybe his presence would keep Chris away,
maybe it wouldn't. Reese really had no idea. He
did know that he obviously enjoyed a round of torture before breakfast because he was in no hurry to
move away from his newly appealing best friend
and get going on his busy day.

Did she always sleep in something so damn…sexy?

Maybe they did need to set some clothing boundaries now that they were temporarily living together.

Their friendship was solid; it was perfect. They completed each other and there was nobody else he would trust with every aspect of his life. But he wasn't quite ready to open up about that letter. He still wasn't sure what to do with the truths it had revealed, and the strange things he was feeling since announcing their fake engagement weren't helping him figure it out.

Only a week ago, his main worry had been about his Manhattan opening and now…well, that opening was the least of his worries. He and his selected launch team had a good handle on the upcoming momentous day and Reese truly believed the opening would be nothing short of a smashing success.

"How's your father?" she asked as she set her mug down. "Still doing good?"

His father. Those two words sounded so odd now, so foreign. He had no idea how he felt about the changes in his family, except maybe a little deceived that the people he'd loved his entire life had lied to him from the beginning.

"Reese?"

He blinked and focused on Josie. "He's fine," Reese replied. "His doctor has checked on him every day since they've been gone."

"That's great. Your mom and dad have worked

so hard and then for him to have heart surgery right after retiring—he deserves some downtime."

Which was one of the reasons Reese had been holding on to this letter, this secret. When the letter came, it had been with a stack of mail that Reese hadn't gotten to immediately. He'd been so swamped with taking over the Conrad restaurants, plus working on the launch of the new one, that if something didn't seem pressing or like an emergency, he'd put it on the back burner.

Josie sighed and came to her feet, bringing his attention back to her.

"I have to finish my article before my noon deadline," she told him. "I'm just going to grab a quick shower first. Feel free to use the guest bath or head on home and get ready there. We can meet up for dinner later if you're free."

She sashayed out of the room…and that was the best way he could describe those swaying hips beneath that flimsy material. It was driving him out of his mind.

He was going to need a shower, too. A very, very cold shower to get control of this new reaction to his best friend, one he should ignore.

Reese cleaned up the few dishes in the kitchen and headed to the spare room to throw on his clothes from yesterday and head to his house for a few things.

As he moved toward his room, he heard a thump

from one of the other guest bedrooms. Then a string of muttered curses followed and Reese let his curiosity get the best of him. He circled back to the nearly closed door and tapped his knuckles on the frame.

"You okay?" he called.

The door flung open and Josie seemed even more frazzled than earlier. A strand of inky black hair fell across her face and she blew it away.

"What are you doing?" he asked, trying to peek over her shoulder.

"Nothing."

Because she tried to slip out the door, Reese took it upon himself to put a hand on the wood and ease it back open.

"You know you're a terrible liar."

He stepped around her and into the room. Simple furnishings with whites and neutrals, a white rug on the hardwood, a sturdy white chair in the corner with a black-and-white-striped pillow.

"Is this where you keep all your journalism secrets?" he joked. "Cocktail recipes or dinner party themes? Am I close?"

"Funny," she mocked, crossing her arms over her chest. "I don't have secrets and even if I did, you would already know them."

The closet door was open just enough for Reese to see a slash of red. Interesting, considering he never saw her in an actual color, let alone something so vibrant.

He moved to the closet and revealed a walk-in space full of the widest variety of colorful clothes he'd ever seen. There were two rows of hanging clothes…all with tags dangling from the sleeves. Boxes of shoes lined the perimeter of the floor and the most insane number of designer handbags in all colors and patterns topped off the high shelves.

Reese glanced over his shoulder, turning his attention to Josie, who glared back at him.

"Opening a department store, Jo?"

She tipped her chin in that defiant way of hers. "No."

"What's with all the brand-new clothes?" he asked, glancing back to the closet that clearly held thousands of dollars' worth of merchandise. "And all this color? Are you giving yourself a makeover?"

Josie's eyes darted to the open room, then down for just a second, but enough for him to see her vulnerability.

"Want to talk about this?" he asked.

She shook her head. "Nothing to talk about. I come in here every morning before I get ready."

"Trying to find something to wear?"

Why was she not just saying whatever she was thinking? For someone who wore black like it was her job, she certainly had a hell of a lot of funds tied up in a brand-new, not-black wardrobe.

"I can't be her," she murmured.

What? What did that even mean? Who couldn't she be?

Forgetting the lame joke he'd been going for when he first saw this shocking surprise, Reese took a step toward her, wondering what she'd been hiding and why she seemed so sad, so…almost helpless.

She'd just told him she didn't keep any secrets, but that had clearly been a lie because all of this was obviously something she wanted to keep to herself. How long had this closet full of color been here? And who couldn't she be like?

"Jo—"

An alarm went off from somewhere in the house. Josie immediately turned from the room. Confused as to what had just happened and what the annoying noise was, Reese followed her. He was tempted to grab something from the newly discovered closet to throw over her excuse for pajamas to conceal that dark skin of hers. Granted, he wasn't covered much, either, but she was a temptation he was having a difficult time resisting.

There was only so much a man could take, but the risk of taking what he suddenly wanted was too much. Their friendship was too special, too perfect the way it was. He couldn't afford for his life to get any messier.

Reese found Josie back in the kitchen tapping

away on her phone and thankfully killing that annoying alarm.

"Sorry," she stated with a smile. "That was my reminder to check my planner."

Reese stared at her as she continued to scroll. "You need a reminder to check your schedule? Isn't that just a given?"

Her eyes darted to his and for the briefest of seconds, that heavy-lidded gaze dipped to his chest. Well, well, well. Even with the caffeine and a somewhat better mood, she wasn't immune to his nakedness.

So now what? There was a sudden sexual pull that confused him, intrigued him…challenged him.

"I have an alarm to remind me about nearly everything," she informed him, setting her cell back on the table and turning to face him fully. "A reminder to drink all my water, feed my plants, check in with my new assistant because she seems a little overwhelmed at times, and—"

Reese held up a hand. "I get it. I knew you were structured, but I had no idea it was to this extent."

Josie smiled. "I can set up your phone so you are more organized with various reminders if you want."

"I've got it all up here," he said, tapping his head. "And my assistant is on everything before I can even think, so I'm good. I wouldn't know what to do with that annoying alarm going off all the time."

"Oh, I have different alarms for different reminders," she countered with a scoff. "I can't have one alarm, Reese. That wouldn't make any sense."

"Of course," he mumbled, then shrugged. "What was I thinking? I guess it's true that you never really know someone until you live with them."

Josie shook her head as she rolled her eyes. "We're not living together. You can go to your place at any time."

"You coming with me?" he asked.

"I'm good here, and Chris is going to be a non-issue," she stated with more confidence than she should have.

Why would Chris give up? Reese sure as hell wouldn't. Josie's ex had had the best woman in the world and he'd let her slip away.

"I'm really going to get a shower now," she told him. "I'm already behind on my morning routine."

As Josie started to pass, Reese took a step to block her. Her hands flew up and flattened on his chest, those dark eyes flashing up to his.

"What's with the closet, Jo?" he asked, really needing to understand what she was hiding, because he'd seen that flash of vulnerability and hurt and he hated knowing she experienced both.

Though it was damn difficult to concentrate with their clothes nearly nonexistent and her hands on his bare skin. Reese had to respect her, respect their friendship and remain in control.

Crossing that invisible barrier into something more intimate would be a mistake. Where had this damn attraction come from? Sexy was one thing, but the ache, the *need* was frustrating.

"Don't worry about the closet," she murmured with a flashing smile. "Why don't you worry about your upcoming restaurant opening instead of me?"

Reese smoothed her hair back from her shoulder, once again torturing himself with the touch of her satiny skin.

"Oh, Conrad's Manhattan is in the forefront of my worries, but what kind of fiancé would I be if I didn't add you to the list?" he joked.

Josie laughed, just as he thought she would, but her eyes dropped to his lips a fraction of a second before she took a step back and sighed.

"You're not my fiancé, Reese. We're just friends."

She licked her lips and blinked as if those last two words were painful to say.

"Just friends," she reiterated beneath her breath as she walked away.

Reese didn't turn to watch her disappear down the hallway. He needed a minute because this morning had been so bizarre. Did Josie have stronger feelings for him than she was letting on? Would she be interested in exploring more with him? And what the hell was up with all of those colorful clothes hanging in the closet with tags?

One thing was certain: now that they were temporarily living together, Reese had to evaluate his feelings and try to figure out what the hell was truly going on between him and his best friend.

Three

Rain pelted down in sheets, right onto Reese. He seriously missed his garage for this very reason. He ran from his SUV to the porch of Josie's beachside home. The second he stepped beneath the shelter, he raked the water from his face. He was absolutely drenched and his overnight bag with dry clothes was in the car because he hadn't wanted to get that soaked as well. He'd just have to dry off and wait out the storm.

He rang the doorbell and glanced in through the sidelight. He didn't see any movement, but surely she was home. He really should've taken that key she'd offered him a long time ago, but why would he have ever had a reason to be here without her?

He rang the bell again and waited. Finally, the lock clicked and the door flew open. Josie stood before him in a black tank and a pair of black shorts, but her hair dripped water droplets onto her shoulders and face and she swiped moisture from her cheeks.

"What the hell happened to you?" he asked.

"There's a leak above my closet," she growled as she turned to race back toward the guest room. "This damn storm."

He closed the door and slid out of his wet shoes so he didn't slide on the tile leading down the hallway. Reese followed her and realized the closet in question was the one with the hoard of colorful clothes. The contents were strewn across the room. Boxes of shoes lay haphazardly along the floor; dresses were in heaps over the chair in the corner and all over the bed. Handbags littered the space around the shoes.

Good grief, there was even more than he'd first realized. How had all of this fit in that space? Granted it was a walk-in closet, but still. Josie really could open a boutique with all of this variety.

Her muttered curse filtered out from inside the closet. Reese stepped in to find her strategically moving buckets beneath the drips.

"Every time I think I have it, another area presents itself," she told him. "I do not have time for this."

"Do you have more buckets?"

She shook her head. "I have vases. There are several on the kitchen island. Just dump the flowers in the trash."

Reese raced from the room and headed to the kitchen where he came to an abrupt stop. The most obnoxious display of flowers covered her entire island. A wide variety of colors and blooms…all fresh and nothing Josie would ever purchase for herself.

No surprise to find cheesy notes attached. Reese made quick work of getting rid of the flowers, then he took armfuls of vases back to the closet.

"Want to discuss this?" Reese asked, holding a vase up and wiggling it.

"Nope."

"You have thousands of dollars' worth of flowers spread across your island."

"Not my money," she said, taking one vase at a time and looking at the ceiling for where to usefully place it. "And before you say anything else, I definitely realize Chris is an issue now."

Well, at least that was something. Chris wasn't going to just slink away. Reese truly believed the man thought he stood a chance at getting Josie back, but that wasn't happening.

"Why did you marry him to begin with?" Reese asked, his thoughts coming out before he could stop himself.

Josie reached for another vase, her dark eyes locking on his for the briefest of moments. "That's a conversation for another time."

And definitely one he would circle back to, because he'd wondered this since the moment she'd dropped the bomb that she'd eloped at the courthouse. The courthouse, for crying out loud.

Josie deserved more than a quickie wedding. He remembered her always talking about wanting a ceremony on the beach, small and intimate. Her love of the beach was just another thing they had in common…granted, he wasn't looking for marriage.

That engagement of his had been a mistake and one he'd likely have to answer for when they circled back to the topic later. Josie deserved an explanation, too.

Reese took the last two vases and looked around, but didn't see any more leaks. He sat them aside and pulled out his cell. Getting his contractor out here as soon as this storm passed was imperative, before any more damage was done.

Minutes later, he disconnected the call and focused back on Josie.

"My guy will be here as soon as he can."

Josie glanced from bucket to bucket to vase. "This place is a mess."

"Have you seen any other leaks?"

Josie's eyes widened and she pushed passed him to exit the closet. In her hurried, frantic state, he assumed that was a no. Whatever room she went into, he looked in another. It didn't take long to find that there were two other small leaks, both in Josie's bedroom.

"This is an absolute nightmare," she sighed once the other vases were in place and they'd gone back into the kitchen.

"It can all be fixed," he assured her. "My guy is the best and once this storm passes, we'll get it taken care of."

Josie pushed her hair from her face and stared at the mess of blooms and greenery. "I do feel bad putting them all in the trash."

"Then don't." Reese reached for one stem and picked it up, examining it before glancing back to Josie. "We can make smaller arrangements and take them to the cardiac unit where Dad was. We could give some to the nursing staff and some to the patients."

Josie granted him the widest, sweetest smile. "I would have never thought of that. You're sweet sometimes, you know."

Reese shrugged, not really needing compliments for just trying to find a solution to this mess.

"He had excellent care there, so maybe these would brighten their day. And I know they always have patients with no family."

"Always thinking of others." Josie reached up and rested her hand on the side of his face. "One day you're going to find the right woman. She's going to be damn lucky."

"You're the only woman who puts up with me," he joked.

She dropped her hand and glanced to the flowers. "Well, you keep up with those sweet gestures and you'll be taken in no time."

Taken. The only place he wanted to be taken was to a bed with Josie. Or here in the kitchen would work.

But Josie had everything and everyone in a particular slot, and he was in the friend zone, which hadn't been an issue…until now. The structure in her life stemmed from her retired military father. Her mother had passed away when Josie was a toddler, so she didn't remember her and Reese had never met the woman.

"I'm not looking for marriage," he stated honestly. "Being engaged was enough of a scare to make me realize I prefer being married to work. That's a relationship I can feed into and grow, not to mention control."

"Ah, yes. Control. Well, that is why you'll always be alone. Women don't want to be controlled," she scolded. "Don't you want to have someone to come home to? Someone to share everything with? Someone to grocery shop with?"

Reese laughed. "First of all, I don't grocery shop. Second, I tell you everything. And when I come home, I have a glass of bourbon. All my bases are covered."

Josie rolled her eyes. "That sounds so lonely."

"And in my defense, I'd never want to control a woman," he told her. "I know not to fight a losing battle."

"You really are a great guy," she stated again.

"Are you vying for a new position?" he asked. "We are engaged, after all."

"We're not engaged," she laughed. "Though I might need to convince Chris you were telling the truth because clearly he didn't believe us or he just doesn't care."

"Or he's an idiot, which is my vote," Reese added. "Pack a bag and come to my place."

Josie's eyes widened. "What? I'm not just coming to your place. My house is falling in, if you haven't noticed."

"Your house isn't falling in. My guy will be here to fix everything and you don't want to be here during that construction anyway." Reese reached for her and raked his thumb over her ring finger. "We need to get a ring."

Josie pulled her hand away and laughed. "Can you focus for two minutes?"

"Oh, I'm focused."

She rolled her eyes and turned her attention back to the flowers. "Let me find some tissue paper and ribbon. I'm out of vases."

"Just gather them all up and we'll find vases at my house," he told her. "Grab a bag of whatever you need to stay the night."

"This is silly, you know." Josie started gathering the flowers. "I can stay here."

"You can, but why?" he countered, helping her gather everything. "We'll do a movie night like we used to."

She stilled and gave him a side-eye. "I get to choose the movie?" she asked.

Reese cringed. "Don't tell me."

Josie squealed and a wide grin spread across her face. "Oh, you know it."

Yeah, he did. Her all-time favorite movie was *An Affair to Remember*. She'd first introduced it to him when they were in high school and he'd absolutely hated it. Since then, any time she chose the movie, that's the one she went with. He didn't hate it now—hell, he could say the thing word for word. If she enjoyed it, that's all that mattered.

"Go pack your stuff and I'll take the flowers," he told her. "I'll meet you at my house."

"Deal."

She practically skipped from the room and Reese couldn't help but feel a niggle of worry deep in his gut. Spending more time alone with Josie had never been an issue before, but his hormones had never entered the picture before, either. At least, not like this. Now she was coming to his house for the night and Reese couldn't help but wonder how much more he could take before he snapped and crossed the line they couldn't come back from.

He was a jumble of nerves—between the mysterious closet she hadn't explained, the letter he'd received and the fact that he wanted Josie more than anything he'd ever wanted.

One night. He just needed to take this fake engagement one night at a time. Surely he could control himself for one night…right?

Josie pulled through Reese's gate and wondered how she'd let him talk her into this. Granted, she hadn't put up much of a fight. She'd been tired, worried about her roof, and she really didn't want to be present when workers started banging around and making more of a mess.

Still. Was he going to parade around in those little black boxer briefs again? True, she'd seen him in swim trunks, but that was before something had shifted in her mind with the words *my fiancé*.

That was before he'd pulled her into his side and caressed her hip like only a lover would do. There was something so possessive, so damn sexy about the way he'd taken charge. Her entire life she'd prided herself on being independent. Yet the way Reese had claimed her had done something to that friend switch and she wasn't sure she could flip it back to the way it used to be…the way it was *supposed* to be.

Ugh. This entire situation had gotten out of control so fast, she was both confused and frustrated. For someone who always had every damn thing in order and under control, her mental state was a complete mess.

Josie pulled around the circular drive and stopped right in front of the steps leading up to Reese's insanely large beach house. The man never did anything in small proportions. His house was easily four times the size of hers and he lived alone. His chef and maid came and went—they were hardly ever seen, yet the house remained immaculate and there were always fresh dishes in the refrigerator.

Reese treated his employees like family and they remained so loyal and went above and beyond to please him. He might be a billionaire mogul, but he was literally the only person she knew with a selfless heart of gold.

Josie's cell chimed just as she put her car into Park. If this was another text from Chris…

She'd totally downplayed how much he'd texted and called because she didn't want Reese to go complete Neanderthal on her…though proclaiming upcoming nuptials had been pretty caveman of him.

She opened the text, relieved to see it was from her editor, Melissa, but that relief quickly turned to dread.

Congrats on the big engagement! We just posted a blog teaser, but I want a Q&A with you and Reese ASAP! This is so exciting!

With her breath caught in her throat, Josie reread Melissa's text. Josie had confided in her assistant, Carrie, earlier that morning, more joking than anything, that Reese had claimed they were engaged and her world had been flipped upside down, but she was still getting that column in on time.

Josie had thought they were just having random chatter and now this? A teaser blog post had already gone up on the site…the site that had hundreds of thousands of hits per day. There was no pulling back from such a dramatic announcement without tarnishing the stellar reputation of not only *Cocktails & Classy*, but of her own image as well.

Josie stared at the message, unsure how to respond. She did, however, know who was responsible for this leak. As if following up with her somewhat new assistant constantly to make sure things were done properly wasn't annoying enough, now she couldn't trust her.

And here they'd thought getting rid of Chris would be the biggest issue.

Obviously, Josie's assistant would have to be dealt with first thing in the morning. Right now, though, she had one other matter to handle.

She had to actually fake an engagement to her best

friend. This had gone beyond just lying to her ex. Now the public was aware of her personal life, too.

Josie hit Reply and chose her words carefully. Thankfully, she wasn't responding in person and dealing with Melissa seeing her shocked face.

Thanks. I had no idea you would find out this way. We're still processing the news, so the Q&A might have to wait.

Josie knew her fans would want the scoop, especially since she was coming off a divorce only six months ago. The outpouring of love and kindness had overwhelmed her and left her feeling a little guilty, considering she hadn't loved Chris. He'd been a nice guy who'd come along at the wrong time. Why wouldn't he just let her set him free?

She prided herself on being available to her readers and really interacting with them, so it was quite understandable that Melissa would want to share the happy news with the world. Unfortunately, the last thing Josie wanted was another public relationship...another *failed* public relationship. Because this fake engagement certainly wasn't going to last.

Josie didn't wait for a reply. She grabbed her purse and suitcase and headed up the steps to the front door. She was going to have to tell Reese about all of this and then she'd have to see how he felt about a real, fake engagement.

Good heavens, he'd probably do something stupid like really go buy her a ring. And knowing Reese, the thing wouldn't be subtle or cheap.

If only she'd kept her mouth shut earlier on the phone. But in her defense, Josie hadn't had any reason not to trust her assistant. And maybe Carrie was just chattering and not thinking when she told Melissa. Still, the lie was out there and Josie was going to have to deal with the consequences.

The front door flew open and Reese reached for her suitcase. Josie jumped back at his abrupt greeting.

"Why didn't you use the elevator?" he scolded. "I would've gotten this for you so you didn't have to lug it up the stairs."

"It wasn't a big deal," she replied as she stepped into the open foyer. "I'm quite capable of carrying my own luggage."

He muttered something about her being stubborn, but she let that roll off. She was well aware of her stubborn side and she wasn't apologetic for it.

"You ready for that movie?" he asked. "We can set up in the theater room or we can go out onto the patio."

The outdoor patio with a viewing screen was quite impressive, but she couldn't focus on the niceties of his house right now. All she could think about was how fast this fire was spreading and who else knew she and Reese were engaged.

"What's wrong?" he asked, reaching for her hand. "Chris—"

"No."

Well, he had texted, but that wasn't the problem.

"Then what is it?" Reese insisted.

Josie smiled and pulled in a deep breath. "How do you feel about picking out that engagement ring?"

Four

Well, that wasn't at all what he'd thought she'd say. She'd been upset earlier when he'd joked about a ring.

"Engagement ring?" he repeated.

Josie pulled her hand from his and sat her purse on the accent table inside the front door. Tucking her hair behind her ears, she turned to face him once again.

"It's a silly story, really," she began with a nervous laugh. "There was some harmless talk, or what I thought was harmless, on the phone with my assistant about Chris and everything that had happened and then the way you got him to leave. You know… by saying we were engaged."

Reese listened, actually rather amused at her jittery state. Something really had her ruffled.

"We talked about work and moved on," Josie added, fidgeting with her hands. "When I pulled in just now, I got a text from my editor congratulating me on the engagement and telling me that she's got a teaser announcement on the blog site and she needs a Q&A from us. All I can figure is my assistant thought I was serious. I mean, I don't know who else would've told my editor and I guess maybe I forgot to mention this info was confidential. I'm sorry this is all just a big mess now."

Reese continued to watch as she twisted her fingers, smoothed her black dress, toyed with her hair again. The woman was a bundle of nerves ready to explode. This faux engagement was quickly getting to both of them. Likely she was stressed because her life wasn't so neat and tidy right now, the way she liked it. And for him...well, he wanted to strip his best friend and feel those curves beneath his touch and he wasn't sure what to do about those feelings. So, yeah, they had one hell of a problem he didn't have time to solve.

"Then we'll get a ring and answer some questions," he told her, shoving aside his lustful thoughts. "Is that all?"

Her eyes widened. "Is that all? That's your response? We're not getting married, Reese. I can't do this again so publicly. I'm freshly divorced from a marriage that never should've happened in the first place and you and I are both public figures. I mean, we're no royal couple, but the media will be interested in this story."

Reese wrapped his arm around her waist and guided her on into the house. As they stepped down into the sunken living area, he tried to figure out how to assure her that everything would be fine.

"Listen," he started, then stopped and turned to face her, placing his hands on her shoulders. "We play the role. Surely we can pretend to like each other."

She glared up at him and met his crooked grin.

"Would you be serious?" she demanded.

He leaned in just a bit more. Her eyes dropped to his lips, but she pulled her gaze back up to his and held steady.

"Oh, I am serious, Jo. We can answer the questions for your editor and make an appearance at my grand opening in two weeks as a couple. We can push through all of that and then figure out what to do after." He smoothed her hair back and framed her face with his hands. "We can always say we split because we realized we were better at being friends. That's very believable because people have already seen us together as friends—they know we already have a relationship."

"But I don't want to fail at something else," she stated. "Not even fake failing."

That's what she was afraid of? Failing? Nothing about faking being in love with him. Interesting.

"You've never failed at anything," he reminded her. "Not even that marriage you ended once you realized it wasn't working. And I sure as hell am not going to let you start now. We've got this. Together."

She closed her eyes and pulled in a breath, her slender shoulders tensed beneath his hands. Reese gave her a reassuring squeeze, needing her to realize he'd never let her get hurt. He was right here by her side.

"Trust me?"

Her lids lifted as she focused on him. Those deep brown eyes staring at him were usually so good at hiding emotions, but not now. He saw the fear, the vulnerability, the concern. He had all of those, too, but he also had faith enough in their relationship that they would make it through anything...even stepping over that invisible line.

The one he'd promised himself not to cross.

Josie ultimately nodded and a wave of relief washed over him. He would care for and protect her at all costs. He could juggle his family, old and new, plus the Manhattan opening, and still make sure Josie came out of all of this unharmed.

With her eyes still locked onto his, physical need consumed Reese. He leaned in closer, never taking his focus from her. Little by little, he closed the distance until his lips were a whisper from hers.

"Wh-what are you doing?"

Barely hanging on by a thread.

"Practicing," he murmured. "We need to be believable in public."

She licked her lips, but since he'd leaned within a breath of her, her tongue brushed across his bottom lip and Reese knew she certainly hadn't meant to.

But whether she'd meant to or not didn't matter. Just that briefest touch of her tongue snapped something in him.

Reese covered her mouth, gently to give her an opportunity to back up and stop if this was something she didn't want. If she stopped, he would have to respect her decision, but now that he'd touched her in such an intimate, non-friend way, he wanted more.

So. Much. More.

Careful not to touch her anywhere else, Reese clenched his fists at his sides. The desire to reach for her, pull her even closer to get the full experience, consumed him, but he couldn't pressure her. As much as he wanted to keep kissing her, to touch her, his first priority was to make her feel secure.

He had to be patient or he'd risk everything they had.

When her lips opened beneath his, Reese took that as the proverbial green light and deepened the kiss. Delicate fingers feathered up his arm and sent shivers racing through him.

When had he last shivered during a kiss?

Never. He didn't get all giddy and shaken just from a kiss. He wasn't some hormonal teenager.

The woman was potent, more so than he ever could have imagined. When Josie let out a little sigh, Reese reluctantly pulled back.

Clenching his jaw, along with his fists, he closed his eyes and thought of anything other than how much he wanted to take her into his room and finish this.

A kiss so powerful without truly touching was only a stepping-stone to something else...and it was that something else he wanted to experience with her.

"What was that?" she murmured, her hands falling away.

Trying to lighten the intense mood, Reese smiled. "A hell of a practice kiss."

He didn't want to expose his true feelings, didn't want her to feel awkward, either. She'd just gotten here and he didn't want to send her running.

Josie took a step back and nodded. "Right. Well, you're a hell of a kisser."

Now how could his ego stay low with that type of a compliment? And how could he not want even more? Just that simple taste had his imagination running even more rampant with endless possibilities.

"Back at ya," he stated with a grin. "I'll get your stuff into a guest room and then we can watch that movie. Which room do you want?"

"Anything with an ocean view," she told him.

Reese nodded and grabbed her suitcase, needing to get a minute to himself to get his head back on straight. As he took the luggage onto the elevator, Reese wondered how the hell he could focus on anything other than that kiss and how soon they would do it again.

Because now that he'd had one taste, he wanted another, and his drive to share more intimacies with her was stronger than ever. Judging from Josie's surprise reaction and then her response, maybe she had similar needs as well.

Focusing on all of this pent-up desire when he had so much else going on should be silly, foolish even, but all he could think about was how powerful it was and how soon he could kiss her again.

An Affair to Remember was not holding her attention and the lack of interest had nothing to do with the fact that she knew each scene word for word. No, her focus was on her still-tingling lips and the man sitting right next to her on the plush sectional sofa. There were plenty of other seats, but here he sat, right by her side.

What the hell had he been thinking, kissing her like that? Touching her with only his lips, yet her entire body had felt that touch. That little niggle of desire he'd launched earlier by claiming her as his fiancée had become something more. She ached with a need she didn't recognize. Never before had a kiss, so simple and sweet, left her wanting to rip someone's clothes off.

But Reese had pulled back and she'd been left with confusion and need.

If that was their practice kiss, she didn't know what would happen if they had to do the real thing for display…this one had felt pretty damn real.

Her cell vibrated against the table and she glanced down at the screen. But it wasn't her phone; it was his. She'd thought for sure it would be Chris again.

Reese leaned forward and grabbed his phone, stared at it for a minute, then muttered something under his breath before firing off a text.

"Everything okay?" she asked.

He shot her a smile and a nod. "Fine. Just work."

"For the Manhattan opening?"

"No, it's about some business I have in Tennessee."

Surprised, she shifted and put her feet up under her on the sofa. "Does this have anything to do with the trip you just got back from, the one you were so secretive about?"

His eyes darted from the television screen to hers. They'd decided to stay in the theater room since the weather was still nasty outside.

When he remained silent, she reached for the remote and paused the movie, instantly silencing the room. She stared at his strong hands still clutching the phone and wondered what secrets he kept locked in there.

Reese blew out a sigh and reached for her hand. The innocent, friendly gesture he'd done so many times before felt oddly different now, after that toe-curling kiss.

This was still her best friend…her best friend turned faux fiancé. But they only had to play the game for a few weeks and then they could go back to being friends in all aspects.

She would ignore that little voice asking if being friends was all she wanted. Could she be fearless for now? Could she let Reese out of the friends box, just a little? If she was honest, she'd been want-ing…something for a long while now, something different…a change. Maybe she could channel her mother's boldness, just for a while. Since none of this would last, maybe she could grab this chance to pretend to be that bold woman she so desperately wanted to be.

She had such mixed feelings about all of this. How would her heart stand up against playing his fiancée, with all the touching and lingering glances? And how would such acts change the dynamics of their entire relationship? Could they easily slide from one type of intimacy to another without any emotional damage?

She wasn't sure. And yet a part of her wanted to find out.

"I'm not purposely keeping anything from you," he finally told her as his thumb raked over the ridges of her knuckles. "Just sorting through some things. I'll fill you in when I'm ready."

Whatever it was sounded serious. Reese was always the good-time guy. The one who pulled her out of her shell and tried to get her to ditch her planner and do something, anything, spur-of-the-moment. So whatever plagued his mind, it was something big.

The way he kept stroking her hand had even more shivers pumping through her and Josie wasn't so sure staying here at his house was a great idea. At least she was not staying in the same room with him. The hour was getting late and she had to start on a new project in the morning. She was going to need a clear mind and not one filled with passionate kisses and unsettling fantasies about her bestie.

"I'm tired," she told him as she eased away and came to her feet. "I have a busy day tomorrow so I'm going to head up to my room."

Reese stood, too, instantly invading her space by his sheer size. She'd always known he was a broad guy—he did value his gym time—but she hadn't realized just how powerful and sexy he appeared until just now. Her heart beat quicker; her body tingled in ways it shouldn't from just looking at her best friend.

"Are you okay?" he asked, his brows drawn in. "If you're worried about the leaks at your place, my contractor will fix everything and you'll never know there was a problem."

Her leaks. Right. She'd honestly forgotten about that particular mess. Pretty much everything pre-kiss had slipped from her mind. Though she really should try to get back to reality because none of this—not what she was feeling, not what they were pretending—was valid.

Those few seconds of connection with Reese weren't real. He didn't want to build anything with her based on that kiss and he'd already told her this was all for show.

Fine. She could deal with that, but she still didn't know how all of this would work. She didn't have another space filed away for him. He was her rock, her very best guy, the one she could go to for anything. Shifting him somewhere else in her life would only unsettle the solid structure she strived for.

If she failed publicly at a relationship again, she worried how her reputation would hold up. She worried she'd let herself down, because she'd always prided herself on her independence and her control. Thanks to her military father and her regimented childhood, she knew no different.

"I'm not worried about the leaks," she assured him.

Reese reached up and tucked a strand of hair behind her ear, then trailed his fingertips down her jawline. Had he always been this touchy? This affectionate? Was Reese's interest recent or had she taken all of those innocent touches for granted before?

"Is it the kiss?" he asked.

Her heart caught in her throat. Leave it to him to draw out the awkwardness and make it bold and commanding.

"We're still friends," he added. "That kiss didn't have to mean anything."

Josie swallowed and went for full-on honesty as she looked him directly in his daring blue eyes. She was drowning and she had no clue how to save herself other than to just get out of the current situation.

"But it did."

Before the moment could get any more awkward or before he replied that he didn't feel anything, Josie turned and left the room. Maybe that made her a coward, but right now, she was afraid. Afraid for what would happen after two weeks of pretending, when she'd only been here two hours and already had stronger feelings than she should. The fear also stemmed from not knowing how much longer Reese could stay in that friend box she'd so carefully packed him in.

But most of all, she worried that she would never be the same because now that she'd had a hint of what Reese could bring out in her...she wanted to experience even more and that revelation would certainly keep her awake all night.

Five

"Is everything okay, son?"

Reese tightened his grip on the steering wheel as his father's voice came over the speaker in his SUV.

Son. The simplest endearment, one Reese had heard countless times over the years, yet the word only reminded him of all the lies he'd been living for nearly forty years.

Reese turned into Conrad's first location in Sandpiper Cove. This place was as old as he was and the most sought-out restaurant in the state. Many magazines and even television shows showcased Conrad's and its specialty menus and fine dining experience.

All of this belonged to Reese now because he was Martin Conrad's son...or so he'd always believed.

But even having this dynasty passed down to him, Reese wanted to build his own legacy, which was why he was getting the next phase going with his opening in New York.

"I'm fine," Reese replied, pulling into his parking spot. "I'm glad you and Mom are having a nice trip. You both deserve the getaway."

And they did. They had worked every single day for as long as Reese could remember, growing this dynasty from a meager savings account that they'd invested in an old shack. All of that blew up into something amazing and the shack remained, but took on renovation after renovation. Surrounding properties were purchased to accommodate the growth and it wasn't long before they realized they should open another restaurant and then another.

Reese was proud to be part of such a hardworking family; they had taught him so many of his core values. He'd always wanted a family of his own, children to pass this legacy down to someday.

But now? Well, now he questioned everything.

"We're having the best time," his father stated. "Wait… What, Laura?"

Reese waited while his parents held their own conversation in the background. Despite everything he'd learned from that letter, and he was still questioning the validity of revelations from a woman he'd never met, Martin and Laura had raised him. They'd loved him and provided for him, so no matter the outcome of their eventual confrontation about his biological father, they were his parents. He just wished like hell they would've trusted him enough to tell him the truth—if there was a truth to tell.

"Engaged?" his father exclaimed. "Reese, your mother says you're engaged? She's reading that blog she loves from Josie's magazine. What, Laura? He's engaged to *Josie*? Our Josie?"

Josie had been part of his family for so long. When her father was out of town working or traveling, Josie tended to land at their house. Most holidays during their college days she had spent with them. She was like the daughter his parents never had.

Reese raked a hand over the back of his neck. Yeah, he probably should have told them about this sooner, like last night, but his mind hadn't been on the fake engagement; it had been on Josie and kissing her and her telling him that the encounter had been much more than a simple kiss. He'd wanted to know exactly what she meant by that.

But she'd walked away.

He'd stood in his theater room staring at the empty doorway long after she'd left. Obviously, he hadn't been the only one affected by the kiss and now he had to figure out what to do with this information.

Still, his parents deserved a heads-up. They truly

loved Josie like their own…and they were clearly thrilled by this unexpected news.

"Son, are you still there?"

Reese pulled himself back to the call. "Yeah. I'm here. And I was going to tell you today, actually. This all happened so fast."

"Josie is such a wonderful girl," his father boasted. "Hold on, your mother wants to talk to you."

Reese swallowed and listened to the static as the phone was passed around, then he was immediately greeted with his mother's high-pitched squeal.

"Darling," she yelled. "I'm so happy for you guys, though I don't know why I had to read about it online instead of hearing the news from my own son. We will discuss that later, but for now I want to know how you feel. Are you excited? How did you propose? I saw this coming years ago. I cannot wait to throw you guys a proper engagement party."

Reese's mind whirled with one question and thought after another. His mother was always all-hands-on-deck. The woman was only "off" when she was asleep. There was no way he could let her start planning an engagement party. She would get way too wrapped up in this and right now, he couldn't share that it was a sham.

"Mom, let's not order any party decorations just yet," he stated. "Josie is swamped with work and I'm busy with the Manhattan opening. Let's get on the other side of these two weeks and then we can talk. Okay?"

Silence on the other end was all the warning he needed to know she did not like his idea.

"I promise," he quickly added. "You know how important this next opening is. I'm starting a new chapter and I need to focus solely on that. Josie completely understands."

"Of course she does," his mom agreed. "That's why the two of you are so perfect for each other. You're both workaholics."

Well, that was definitely true. Reese took after his father—well, after Martin. He devoted nearly every moment to making sure their upscale restaurants maintained the highest prestige and top-notch reputation people had come to appreciate from them.

"I've asked Josie to cover the event, too," he quickly told her, turning the conversation toward business. "I figure since she's going as my date, and there's no one else I'd rather give an inside scoop to, this would be a win-win for everyone."

"I can't wait to see you guys," she exclaimed. "You give Josie a big hug and kiss from me."

A hug and a kiss? Sure, no problem. Everything else that came to mind? Yeah, that was the problem.

"We will see you at the opening," she told him. "Love you, Reese."

Emotions threatened to overtake him, but he tamped them down. His mother did love him, that was never in question. But at some point, he'd have to find the right words and the right time to question them.

"I love you, Mom. See you in two weeks."

After Reese hung up, he sat alone with his guilt and tried to tell himself this situation wouldn't last long. Two weeks and he and Josie would go back to being friends. Nobody had to know this had all been a sham, not even his parents.

But he would know.

Every part of him wondered how the hell he could go back to never touching her, never kissing her the way he truly wanted.

And he knew she was affected, too. He'd seen that flare in her eyes and heard that swift intake of breath.

Reese's cell chimed in his hand before he could exit his SUV. He glanced down to the screen to see a message from Josie.

Melissa wants a photo shoot along with the Q&A. She has it all scheduled for tomorrow morning at nine and is hoping to use Conrad's as the backdrop. Want me to make an excuse to postpone?

Reese stared at the message. If they kept pushing forward, how much damage would be done in the end?

But, really, what would a few pictures hurt? The

Q&A wouldn't be a big deal. They knew each other better than they knew themselves at times. And the coverage might be good for his new opening, too.

No big deal. We can all meet at the restaurant.

She instantly replied back.

I'm sorry about all of this.

He blew out a sigh and hit Reply.

I'm sorry, too. We'll get through this together.

There was only one thing in his entire life he was afraid of and that was losing Josie forever. Even with everything going on around him, he couldn't lose her. The risk of seeking something more with her terrified him, but he was starting to believe that if he never tried, that would terrify him more.

What if he didn't lose her friendship? What if something magical developed? If he didn't test these new feelings, his fear of the unknown could rob him of the chance at something good.

But… Having a committed relationship really wasn't something he had the time for right now. He was just getting started on this new chapter in his career, and he needed to devote every bit of energy and time to making this next phase a success.

Not only did he demand that of himself, he also didn't want to let his parents down. They'd entrusted their dynasty to him and he'd be damned if he'd get sidetracked.

Reese shot off another reply to Josie.

See you at home tonight.

The message went before he realized how familial that sounded. He certainly wasn't ready for all of that. Maybe someday, but not now. He was too slammed with work and the fact that his personal life from all angles had taken drastic turns.

Yet he couldn't deny he liked knowing Josie would be at his house waiting on him. He'd already asked his chef to prepare Josie's favorite meal and dessert. There was a bottle of her favorite wine chilling and he intended to make this very stressful situation as relaxing as possible for both of them.

Reese stepped from his car and into the hot summer sun that was already beating down. Every single day he came to Conrad's when he was in town, but today he had the urge to blow off work and hit the beach like normal people. He wondered if Josie would ever consider doing something that spontaneous, that out of the ordinary, something that wasn't already scheduled in her planner.

Reese stepped in through the back door, disarmed the alarm and headed for the office he kept on the top floor. The second floor was for VIP guests only and that lounge area was consistently booked. But Reese kept his office on the top floor away from the noise and confusion where he could really work and continually design new ways to grow the company.

As soon as he stepped off the elevator, he pulled up Josie's text again and replied. Tomorrow was a special day and he didn't want it marred by the black cloud of deceit hanging over their heads.

Take the rest of tomorrow off after the Q&A and photo shoot. I have a surprise.

He knew what her response would be. He knew exactly what she'd send back before he even glanced at his screen. So when the phone vibrated in his hand with a new message, he laughed.

I hate surprises. I need to plan what I'm doing. It's like you don't know me.

Oh, he knew her, which was exactly why he wanted to push her beyond her comfort zone, see her live a little. They were both stressed and a day off would do them good. No, he didn't have the time to take off, but nothing was more important than Josie.

Besides, tomorrow was her birthday and he would surprise her with whatever the hell he wanted.

He didn't respond to her message; he just decided

to let her think about all the possibilities he might have in store. She'd mentioned working from home today, his home, not hers since there was a crew already at her place working on the damaged roof. He'd already told his chef, Frisco, to take extra special care of Josie and to make sure she was comfortable.

Having her at his house seemed strange, yet right. Reese couldn't help but wonder how she felt being there after last night.

Reese planned on discussing that kiss with her again, finding out exactly how she felt…because he wanted more. More kisses, more touches…just more of Josie, and now that she was in his home, he had the opportunity…but should he take it?

Six

Josie finished her work, leaned back in the chair and stared at the screen. Something felt so off, but she just couldn't put her finger on it. Having an empty wineglass wasn't helping.

It grated that her entire work mode could be tilted off-balance because she'd kissed her best friend. No, he'd kissed her…she'd just enjoyed the hell out of it and still felt the tingling on her lips.

With a sigh, Josie came to her feet and closed her laptop. Thankfully, this piece on new summer cocktails wasn't due for another week. She had all the makings for an amazing article. She even had in-spiration photos from the art department with oversize martini glasses filled with pale pink drinks and floating flowers. The recipes shared from various coastal restaurants around the world were in, interviews with restaurant owners were done…but she couldn't find that hook that made everything just come together in an article that didn't sound like a rookie wrote it.

Josie picked up her empty wineglass and left the office. Reese had three designated spots in his home for work and all of them faced the ocean, but she'd chosen the smallest because she preferred to be cozy and quaint…a tough feat in a house of this magnitude.

The moment she hit the top of staircase, a delicious aroma wafted up from the first floor. The chef had only made his presence known once and that was to ask her what she wanted for her lunch. Josie was so used to making her own things or grabbing something from a seaside café that she might get spoiled if she hung around Reese's house too long.

Whatever Frisco had made for dinner smelled like it was going to be divine. The hint of something with peaches hit her as well. There was no way Josie could ever be that masterful in the kitchen; her skills were relegated to her keyboard.

The second she reached the bottom of the steps, Reese walked in the front door. His eyes locked onto hers and Josie gripped the wineglass as she froze. She hadn't seen him since last night, since she fled the room after he'd kissed her. Likely he wasn't awake all night replaying that moment; at least, he didn't look haggard.

That bright blue button-up, folded up on his forearms, showed off not only his tanned skin, but also that excellent muscle tone she knew he worked hard to maintain.

Damn, that kiss had changed everything.

"Looks like you need a refill." Reese broke the silence as he nodded to her glass. "And dinner smells amazing, so this is perfect timing."

He closed the door and tossed his keys onto the accent table before crossing the foyer. Those cobalt-blue eyes locked onto hers and she would have sworn they were more intense than ever.

Yes, that kiss had changed everything.

She'd thought their dynamics had changed with his fake engagement, that first embrace at her door, but that was nothing compared to having his lips on hers. She couldn't seem to put him back in the friends-only box.

Josie had always noticed Reese's striking features and the beauty of his gaze, but she'd never *felt* it before. Josie couldn't begin to share with him what he was doing to her, not when she couldn't even explain all of this to herself.

"I just finished my article," she told him, trying to have what should be a normal conversation. "It's not where I want it, but I can't think anymore today."

Reese reached for her glass. "Let's go have dinner and you can bounce your problems off of me."

Her problems? That was quite laughable considering *he* was the problem. Well, not him physically. No, physically he was the answer, but that was the problem.

Ugh. She was such a mess with her mixed emotions and wayward thoughts. She knew what she meant, but trying to categorize all of her views was proving to be impossible. Josie didn't care for this out-of-control feeling or not being able to maintain some regulation over her own life.

"I'd rather you tell me what's going on tomorrow," she countered, coming down off that last step.

Reese laughed as he started guiding her toward the back of the house. That hand on the small of her back seemed too intimate, but just days ago that would've merely been his friendly gesture. Now she questioned everything…including these newfound emotions.

"We're doing the thing for your magazine and then I have a surprise."

Josie rolled her eyes as she came to a stop. Turning to face him, she crossed her arms over her chest.

"That thing?" she repeated. "You can't be that relaxed about an interview and photo shoot for this fake engagement."

"I'm not relaxed," he amended. "But it's scheduled and there's nothing we can do to change that."

She could call the whole thing off. She could come clean to her boss, just tell her it's a farce, but that would only damage her credibility. If she were going to reveal the truth, she should've done so right off the bat.

"Oh, my mom and dad are thrilled, by the way," Reese added.

Josie gasped. "You told your parents?"

"You know my mother reads your *Cocktails & Classy* blog every single day. I didn't think to warn them off ahead of time."

Guilt overwhelmed her. Josie closed her eyes, pulling in a much-needed deep breath. This lie was spiraling out of control faster than she could keep up. She truly loved and respected Martin and Laura Conrad. What would they think of her after she and Reese "broke up"?

"Hey," Reese said in that calming tone of his. "This is all going to work out. We just need a couple weeks of make-believe and then we're back to being friends and nobody has to know otherwise."

Two weeks might as well be two years or two decades. With the way she was feeling right now, the end result of this charade would be that she'd possibly get intimately attached; her heart might get even more involved, because she didn't know if she'd have the willpower to put a stop to this madness.

Josie focused back on Reese. "Two weeks," she sighed. "We can do this."

The smile that spread across his face packed a punch and she forced herself to return the gesture. Who knew one kiss could cause so many emotions?

"I believe you said something about refilling my wine?"

He nodded and gestured for her to go ahead. "I had my chef make all of your favorites for dinner, so I hope you didn't have a big lunch."

Josie laughed. "He tried to feed me a five-course meal at noon."

"I told him to make sure you were well-fed and taken care of."

Taken care of. That's exactly what Reese lived for. He was always taking care of his parents, taking care of his staff of hundreds, taking care of her. He was the most selfless, giving man.

Before that kiss, those selfless traits were just part of what she'd loved about him as her friend. But now…well, she couldn't help but wonder how that generosity would carry over into the bedroom.

The instant mental image had her stilling, fantasizing for just a moment. Then she crashed back to reality as she refocused on Reese's gaze.

"I would've been fine with a banana or a smoothie," she told him. "But I appreciate it."

They stepped into the vast kitchen with views of the ocean through the windows, which stretched across the entire back wall. The sun was starting to set, casting an orange glow over the horizon and making the bright blue water sparkle like diamonds.

A million-dollar view.

Josie turned her attention to the long island and nearly gasped. "What is all of this?"

Reese laughed as he went to the wine fridge at the end of the island. "Dinner."

"For all of Sandpiper Cove?" she asked, her eyes scanning each dish.

"I told Frisco to prepare all your favorites and I gave him a list."

And from the looks of things, Reese hadn't missed a thing. There was even a little bowl of Tootsie Rolls, which made her laugh.

"How in the world did he pull off all of this?" she asked. "And the lunch he prepared was insane."

Reese shrugged. "That's why I can never let him leave me. I'd starve, and he's a magician when he's in his element."

Her eyes locked onto his. "You know we can't possibly eat all of this, right?"

"Of course not," he agreed. "Frisco always takes any extras to the homeless shelter, so I don't mind that he goes all out. I know none of this will actually go to waste."

Flowers to the hospital, food to the homeless shelter. Seriously, her best friend was not a typical jet-setting billionaire. She'd always admired his giving nature, or maybe it was that she'd just not seen him in this light before. Because the fact that he always put others first was becoming sexier and sexier.

"What's that smile for?" he asked.

She circled the island and placed a hand over his heart. "You're just remarkable. I mean, I've always known, but lately you're just proving yourself more and more."

He released the wine bottle and covered her hand with his...and that's when the memory of that kiss hit her again, hard. She shouldn't have touched him. She should've kept her distance. Because there was that look in his eyes again.

Where had this come from, this pull between them? When did he start looking at her like he wanted to rip her clothes off and have his naughty way with her?

"We need to talk about it," he murmured.

It.

As if saying the word *kiss* would somehow make this situation weirder. And as if she hadn't thought of anything else since *it* happened.

"Nothing to talk about," she told him, trying to ignore the warmth and strength between his hand and his chest.

"You can't say you weren't affected."

"I didn't say that."

He tipped his head, somehow making that penetrating stare even more potent. "It felt like more than a friendly kiss."

Way to state the obvious.

"And more than just practice," he added.

Josie's heart kicked up. They were too close, talking about things that were too intimate. No matter what she felt, what she thought she wanted, this wasn't right. She couldn't ache for her best friend in such a physical way. If that kiss changed things, she couldn't imagine how much anything more would affect this relationship.

How could she maintain control of her emotions if she let this go any further? She was already having a difficult enough time trying to cope with the current circumstances.

"We can't go there again," she told him. "I mean, you're a good kisser—"

"Good? That kiss was a hell of a lot better than just good."

She smiled. "Fine. It was pretty incredible. Still, we can't get caught up in this whole fake engagement thing and lose sight of who we really are."

His free hand came up and brushed her hair away from her face. "I haven't lost sight of anything. And I'm well aware of who we are...and what I want."

Why did that sound so dangerous in the most delicious of ways? Why was her body tingling so much from such simple touches when she'd firmly told herself not to get carried away?

Wait. Was he leaning in closer?

"Reese, what are you doing?" she whispered, though she wasn't putting up a fight.

"Testing a theory."

His mouth grazed hers like a feather. Her knees literally weakened as she leaned against him for support. Reese continued to hold her hand against his chest, but he wrapped the other arm around her waist, urging her closer.

There was no denying the sizzle or spark or whatever the hell was vibrating between them. She'd always thought those cheesy expressions were so silly, but there was no perfect way to describe such an experience.

And kissing her best friend—again—was quite an experience.

Reese deepened the kiss, parting her lips and exploring further. She'd stop him in just a minute—she just wanted a little more.

Josie slid her hand from his and gripped each side of his face as he leaned her back a little more. That strong arm across her lower back held her firmly in place. Threading her fingers through his hair, she tilted her head to give him even more access, but those talented lips trailed across her jaw and down the column of her neck.

Any second she should end this, but it felt so damn good she couldn't muster up the strength to tell him to stop. She also couldn't remember why this was such a bad idea.

That hand behind her started shifting; a thumb slid beneath the hem of her shirt and caressed her bare skin. Josie let out a moan, then quickly bit down on her lip to quiet herself. Reese's lips continued to explore her neck, the sensitive spot behind her ear, then down into the vee of her shirt.

There were too many clothes in the way. Her body ached like it never had before and she wanted to feel his skin against hers.

"Reese," she panted, though she didn't know what she was begging for. She just knew she wanted him to keep going, to keep making her feel everything she'd deprived herself of.

An alarm echoed in the room, but Josie ignored it. She didn't want this moment to end…at least not yet.

But the insistent beeping kept going. Reese rested his forehead against her shoulder and she noted his body trembling just as much as hers…if not more.

"I have to get that," he murmured.

Get what? Her mind was still spinning and she didn't know what the noise was, but she wanted it to go away.

Reese slowly released her, holding her steady until she looked up at him and nodded. Her legs weren't quite as steady as she would've liked, so she rested a hand on the edge of the island and willed herself into a normal breathing pattern and heart-beat.

When Reese grabbed his cell from his pocket,

Josie realized that hadn't been an alarm at all, but a call. Maybe the interruption was a blessing, because she still wasn't convinced she could have stopped what had been about to happen...and she was already wondering when it would happen again.

Seven

Reese cursed the caller before even looking at the screen. He needed to get in control and back to reality before answering, but he was having a difficult time with that considering he could still feel Josie's sweet body beneath his touch.

Damn it, how far would he have taken things? How far would she have allowed this to go?

Glancing down at the screen, he saw Sam Hawkins's name.

Sam Hawkins, the man who was very likely Reese's half brother and one of the men Reese had gone to see last week. The owner of Hawkins Distillery in Green Valley, Tennessee, was a pretty remarkable guy, considering he was the youngest distiller in the country.

Reese glanced to Josie, who was staring down at the floor, her eyes wide with shock. He wasn't sure if she was shocked over their behavior or shocked over the fact that she'd enjoyed it so much—because those pants and moans and the way she'd clutched his hair were all clear indicators she'd been more than eager for things to progress.

Turning from temptation, Reese answered the call.

"Hello?"

"Reese," Sam responded. "I hope this isn't a bad time."

Bad time? Reese supposed it could've been worse—like if Sam had called in about ten minutes when clothes were strewn across the floor.

He looked again at Josie, who still seemed to be trying to catch her breath. Yeah, same here. He'd only meant to see if the effect of the kiss last night had been a onetime occurrence, but the moment his lips touched hers, there had been another internal snap that he couldn't control.

"Now is fine," he replied, focusing on the sunset outside instead of the beauty before him. "I didn't expect to hear from you so soon."

"I know. Nick and I were going to give you some time to process everything," Sam stated. "Especially considering you don't know Rusty like we do, it's still a shock to discover your father at our age."

Understatement. Reese hadn't even known there was a father to discover. He thought Martin Conrad *was* his father, for nearly four decades.

"Since Rusty is home from his stint in jail for embezzling from one of our local charities, Nick and I planned on confronting him with the truth."

Reese was well aware that Rusty had been arrested for skimming funds from a charity that Lockwood Lightning endorsed and supported. From all the stories Reese had heard and from the bits and pieces of what he'd dug up online, Reese had drawn his own conclusions that he'd lucked out in life by not having Rusty Lockwood raise him as his child.

"And you want me in on that meeting?"

Reese had to choose his words carefully because he still hadn't explained everything to Josie—they'd sort of been busy pretending to be engaged, fighting a magnetic attraction—and he still wasn't sure how the hell to handle any of this.

"We don't want to pressure you, but I did want to include you," Sam told him. "All of this is still new to us as well. I wouldn't mind getting to know my half brother a little more, but that's going to be your decision."

Half brothers. Reese had grown up an only child and used to wonder how having a sibling would've changed his life. He likely would've been sharing the family business. Having someone else to lighten the load wouldn't be a bad thing. He would've had an automatic friend growing up, too, but he'd had plenty of friends even without siblings.

Friends like the one he'd just groped until she was moaning in pleasure.

Pushing aside those delicious thoughts of Josie, Reese focused on what he wanted to know about Nick and Sam. Discovering two guys who were prominent in their fields of luxury liquor and hospitality—fields surprisingly similar to his own—and who were both eager to get to know him sounded promising, and Reese found that he did want to explore these new relationships.

This whole new chapter in his life would take some time to wrap his mind around, but new ventures never scared Reese. He welcomed challenges… including kissing Josie Coleman.

Again, he shifted his focus back to the call and away from Josie.

"I could make another trip to Green Valley," he told Sam. "Why don't you tell me when would work for you guys? I'm opening a new restaurant in Manhattan next weekend. Maybe we could discuss a possible working relationship as well."

"That would be a solid start," Sam agreed. "I'll talk with Nick and text you. We plan on confronting Rusty soon, though."

Reese swallowed and wondered if tag-teaming

was the answer. What good would come from all of them going to Rusty? What did Sam and Nick hope to accomplish? Did they just want to let the mogul know that his sons had all been identified?

None of them needed money and Reese certainly wasn't looking for a father figure to fill a void. He had plenty of love and affection from the amazing couple who'd raised him.

Reese really needed to talk to his own parents before he went to Rusty. He needed all of the history, no lies, no secrets. Reese needed every bit of his life revealed to him.

He needed to understand his true role when it come to Rusty Lockwood. He needed to know where he actually stood in all of his relationships and what the hell he was supposed to feel.

Because his entire world was in upheaval and he honestly had no idea what to think about any of it.

"I'll see what I can work out," Reese replied. "But I can't make promises right now."

"Understood. I'll be in touch soon."

Reese disconnected the call, held his cell at his side and continued to stare out the window. He wasn't ready to face Josie yet, not when his body was still humming from their brief, intense encounter. Their clothes had stayed on. There had barely been any skin-on-skin contact. What would happen when they finally took that next step?

Because Reese had every intention of doing just

that. He'd been uncertain before, even after that first kiss, but the way she'd responded moments ago—how could he deny either of them?

There was too much passion here to ignore. There was too much pent-up desire. Who knew how long those feelings had been stirring?

They would never know what they could have if he didn't take the risk. No, he didn't want to lose her as his best friend, but what if things only got better?

When he turned, he found Josie staring straight at him. She'd clearly had time to compose herself, but that hunger was still in her eyes. Her squared shoulders and tight lips, though, were good indicators that she wasn't happy about what she was feeling.

"You're going back to Green Valley?" she asked.

Reese pocketed his phone. "That's not where I thought we'd pick up from where we just left off."

She crossed her arms and stared across the room. "Where did you think we'd pick up? Kissing? Because I'm still not sure that's a good idea."

And that's where they clearly disagreed. There wasn't a better idea, in his opinion.

"You weren't complaining a minute ago," he reminded her—just in case she'd forgotten. "In fact, you were enjoying yourself, if I recall."

Her gaze darted away for a split second before she glanced back to him. "A minute ago, I was sidetracked by, um…"

"My slick moves?" he asked with a smile.

Her eyes narrowed. "Does your ego need to be stroked? I could've kissed anyone and gotten carried away. My eyes were closed, you know, and I happen to like kissing."

Jealousy consumed him as he closed the distance between them. He had her wrapped in his arms and falling against his chest. Her hands flattened on him as her focus was directed straight at his face.

"You think you'd react that way to just anyone?" he asked, tipping her back just enough so she had to cling to him. "Don't throw other men in my face, Josie. I might prove you wrong."

"But…we're friends, Reese."

Something in him softened at her tone, which was laced with confusion—as well as curiosity and desire.

"We *are* friends," he murmured, closing the space between their lips. "Very, very good friends."

Because this was Josie, he wanted to take it slow. He wanted her to recognize this insistent attraction and come to terms with the fact that they had already crossed the friend line. They might as well fully explore this passion.

True, everything surrounding them was in total chaos. But if they didn't take the chance now when they were thrown together, then when would they?

"Reese."

His name slid through her lips as she closed her eyes and tipped her mouth to his. As if he needed any more invitation than that to claim what he so desperately ached for.

Reese wanted her out of this little black dress, he wanted her hair messed up, and he wanted to be the cause of every bit of her chaotic, sexy state.

He'd never wanted a woman so bad in his life.

Her hands came up to his shoulders; her fingertips dug in. Didn't she know? He'd never let her fall.

Reese lifted her up firmly against his body as he spun her around and sat her on the edge of the table. She eased from his kiss and locked her gaze with his. He waited for her to stop him, all the while praying she'd let him continue. Touching her was like a drug he hadn't known he was addicted to and now he couldn't get enough.

He reached up to the strap of her dress and eased it down her arm, taking her bra strap with it. Josie trembled beneath his touch and he had to force himself to keep this slow pace. She wanted him, wanted this—that much was evident in her heavy-lidded stare and flushed cheeks. Not to mention she wasn't telling him no.

Keeping his attention on hers, Reese slid the other straps down, earning him a swift intake of her breath as she raked her tongue across her lower lip. There was no way she could imagine the potent spell she held over him—he hadn't even been sure of it himself until now.

Josie shifted and braced her hands on the table

behind her, quirking a brow as if daring him to stop. Damn, this woman was silently challenging him in the most delicious way.

Reese started to lean in, more than eager to get his lips on that velvety skin of hers.

"Reese," she whispered.

He stopped, his hands braced on either side of her hips.

"As much as we both want this, tell me it won't change things."

The plea in her tone, in her eyes, had Reese swallowing the truth—because things had already changed. The dynamics of their relationship had started changing the moment he knew he wanted her, which, if he was honest with himself, was years ago. She was just finally starting to catch up.

"You'll still be my best friend," he answered truthfully.

He settled his lips over hers as he grazed his hand up her bare thigh and beneath the hem of her dress. She shifted and rocked back and forth slightly to give him better access.

There was nothing he wanted more than to pleasure her right now. To pour out all of the passion he'd been storing up just for her. No woman could ever compare to Josie—which was why he refused to lose her in his life. Yes, intimacy would change things, but maybe it would make them even closer.

Reese feathered his fingertips along the seam of

her panties, earning him a soft moan and a tilt of her hips. But the moment he slid a finger beneath the silky material, he was the one eliciting a moan.

Josie leaned further back, dropping down to her elbows, but still keeping her eyes on his hand. He'd never seen a sexier sight than what was displayed before him. With her hair a mess, her dress hanging on by the curve of her breasts, those expressive eyes silently begging for more and her spread thighs, Reese didn't think he'd be able to ever have a meal at this table again without getting aroused.

As much as he wanted to roam his mouth over all of that exposed skin, he didn't want to miss one second of the desire in her expression. The moment he slid one finger over her heat, Josie's eyes fluttered closed and her mouth dropped open on a gasp.

Yes. That's what he wanted. That sweet, vulnerable reaction.

Finally, Josie eased back all the way and arched her body as she reached down and circled his wrist with her delicate fingers. Relinquishing control was not his go-to, but he was more than willing to let her guide her own pleasure.

It wasn't long before those hips pumped harder against his hand, before she cried out his name and clenched her grip a little tighter.

Reese took it all in. The passion, the need, the completely exposed way Josie let herself be consumed by her desire.

He'd never forget this moment, not for the rest of his life.

When Josie relaxed against the table and released his wrist, Reese eased his hand away and adjusted the bottom half of her clothing. She'd gone totally limp and he couldn't help but smile. He'd never seen her so calm, not worried about a schedule or making plans for something else. She was still, quiet… and utterly breathtaking.

As much as he wanted to use her release as a stepping-stone to more, Reese gathered her in his arms and lifted her against his chest. Her head nestled against the crook of his neck like she'd done so a thousand times before.

Reese lifted her bra straps back into place and adjusted the top of her dress.

Josie's hands reached for the zipper on his pants.

"Not now," he murmured, placing a kiss on the top of her head.

Such an innocent gesture when the most erotic thoughts were swirling through his head. Just knowing she wanted to keep going was a victory he hadn't known was even possible. But she was coming off a euphoria she hadn't anticipated and he didn't want her to think he assumed or expected her to reciprocate.

Josie lifted her head, her tranquil gaze locked on his. "Why?"

He said nothing, but he also wasn't ready to just

let her go. Gathering her up, he crossed to the wall of glass doors and eased one open with his foot.

"Where are we going?" she asked, looping her arms around his neck.

"You're going to sit out here and relax and I'm going to bring you food."

When he placed her on the cushioned chaise in the outdoor living area, she simply stared up at him with her brows drawn.

"That's what you're worried about? Food?"

"Oh, I'm not worried," he corrected. "You haven't had dinner."

She blinked and then shook her head and muttered something under her breath about men being more confusing than women. That was an argument he was smart enough to walk away from.

Leaving her outside, Reese went back into the kitchen, and his gaze kept wandering to the now-empty table. Yeah, he'd never be able to eat there again without thinking of her as she'd just been, and he sure as hell wasn't about to tell his chef what had happened in his kitchen.

Reese turned back to the island, rested his hands on the edge and dropped his head between his shoulders. He just needed a minute to get control over his emotions and his arousal. Turning down her advance had been the most difficult thing he'd ever done, but he wanted the time to be right, for her to come to him because that's what she truly wanted and not because she was fuzzy-headed from a recent orgasm.

When he glanced back up, he caught her gaze staring back at him from where she remained outside. There was a vast distance between them, but he recognized so much in her eyes that he couldn't deny. Along with confusion and a hint of frustration, he still saw passion and he wondered exactly what she planned to do about it.

Eight

Josie stepped out onto the balcony off her guest room. The moonlight cast a bright, sparkling glow over the ocean. She had no clue how long she'd been standing out here letting her thoughts roll through her mind.

Chris had texted only a little while ago and she'd finally responded, telling him this was her final correspondence, she had moved on and she wished the best for him. Then she blocked his number.

She didn't know what to make of everything that had happened earlier with Reese and she couldn't worry about Chris's feelings at this point. It was her slipup on the phone with him that had started this entire ordeal and toppled her life out of control.

All of those neat, tidy boxes that had compartmentalized every aspect of her life were now completely obliterated.

From the way Reese made her feel, to the fact that she'd never felt such a rush of emotions, to the way he'd eased back when she'd reached for him. Everything was different now and she had no idea how she could juggle all of these feelings and still remain calm.

Josie crossed her arms and rubbed her hands over her skin. The breeze off the ocean washed over her, tickling her and doing nothing to dampen her arousal.

And she was still aroused. True, Reese had brought her to pleasure, but she wanted more. He'd left her wondering what else she could experience with him. What would happen if they managed to get all of their clothes off? If they were skin to skin and not worried about anything else beyond physical intimacy?

How would this change their relationship?

Not only that, if she completely let go and gave in to her desires, there would certainly be no controlling where it led. She'd never felt like she was floundering before, but that's exactly where she was right now. The decisions she should make collided with the decisions she *was* making and all of it was confusing the hell out of her.

A sickening feeling settled deep in her stomach over the possibility of losing her very best friend. She couldn't afford to be without him. She couldn't imagine even one day without texting or talking to him. He literally knew her secrets; he was her go-to for everything.

And he'd made her eyes roll back in her head and her toes curl with a few clever touches as he'd laid her out on his kitchen table.

Shivers racked her body as she recalled every talented trace of those fingertips. Who knew her best friend had such moves? And who knew she'd love it so damn much?

Dinner earlier had been strained. Josie wasn't sure if things were awkward because she was still aroused or because their relationship had shifted so far away from something she could recognize and label.

Regardless, Reese and his chef had outdone themselves with all of her favorites. She only wished she could've enjoyed them more.

Josie turned back toward her room and closed the patio doors at her back. She had to get up early and look refreshed for her Q&A and photo shoot. Considering it was well after midnight, she wasn't sure how fresh she would be able to make herself.

There was only so much carefully applied concealer could do.

The silk of her chemise slid over her skin as she padded her way back to her bed. Every sensation since she'd felt Reese's touch only reminded her of how amazing he'd been. Every moment since her release, she'd ached for more and didn't know how to make that happen.

But didn't she know? She was just as much in charge of what was going on as he was.

But was she as brave? Nothing scared or worried Reese. That was the main area where they were 100 percent opposite.

In that kitchen earlier, though, they had been completely and utterly perfect.

Except for that one-off with Chris, Josie had never done something so spontaneous in her life. She made plans for everything and typically got irritated when her plans were shifted or canceled. Some might have even called her a nerd, but she preferred to be described as "structured."

Right now, though, she preferred to finish what Reese had started. Or maybe she'd started this? Regardless of who'd started what, the fact was, nothing had been finished.

And maybe she opted to break out of her perfect box because Reese made her feel things she'd never felt before. Maybe, if she was being honest with herself, she liked experiencing her reckless side with him because she knew she was safe. Reese would never let her get hurt.

Was he in his room thinking about what happened or was he fast asleep without a care? Knowing Reese, he'd fallen right to sleep, and she wasn't even a thought in his mind right now.

Well, too bad, because there was no way she could ignore this and certainly no way she could go to the Q&A and photo shoot while feeling such turmoil.

She didn't know if she was making the best decision or the biggest mistake.

There was only one way to find out.

Arousal and nerves clashed inside her as she tiptoed down the hallway toward Reese's bedroom.

This was insane, right?

She should just go back to her room, read a book or play on her phone or anything until she could push him from her mind.

But one step led to another and she found herself standing outside the double doors leading to the master suite. Josie placed her hands on the knobs and eased the doors open. Moonlight flooded the room, cascading a beam directly onto the king-size bed across from her.

She couldn't do this. She shouldn't be here.

What was she thinking? This was Reese. Her very best friend from school who had seen her at her absolute worst—when her prom date dumped her, when she had that dumb idea to get a perm and he told her she was beautiful anyway, when she broke out in hives from some new facial cleanser she'd tried for an article and he ordered in dinner so she didn't have to go out in public.

He was her rock, her support…not her lover.

Josie turned back toward the hall.

"Stay."

The word penetrated the darkness and had Josie reaching to grip the doorknob again for support. Her heart beat so fast, so hard in her chest, unlike anything she'd experienced before.

"I shouldn't be here," she murmured, still facing the darkened hall. Too late to slip out now.

"You want to be here or you would've stayed in your room."

Why was he always right?

"That doesn't mean this is a good idea," she told him.

The sheets rustled behind her and Josie pulled in a deep breath, willing herself to finish what she'd come for. This was what she wanted; this was exactly why she'd made that short trip from her room to his.

He knew full well why she'd come, so denying it now would only make her look like a fool.

Josie turned, not at all surprised to see Reese standing behind her. Bare chest with a sprinkling of hair, broad shoulders, his dark hair messed up from his pillow and those hip-hugging black boxer briefs were not helping her resolve.

"Who's to tell us this is a bad idea?" he countered in that husky tone of his.

Well, no one really, but shouldn't she be the one saying this wasn't smart? Shouldn't she insist that they were friends above all else?

Yet she'd come to his room because she wanted to forget that common sense logic and remember exactly how amazing she'd felt in his kitchen.

"Stay."

He repeated the simple command, and something just clicked in place—something she hadn't necessarily planned or given much thought to. For the first time in her life, she didn't care about her plans. She only cared about her wants.

And she wanted Reese.

Everything about this felt out of control, and yet safe at the same time.

That moment when she took a step forward, she saw Reese's shoulders relax, a smile spread across his face. There was something so intimate and arousing about the darkness, the quiet of the night and the moonlight streaming through the windows. There was no need to even pretend she didn't want to be here. It was time she owned up to exactly what she needed and not make excuses or apologies.

When this was over, there would be no room for regrets. Regrets would only lead to the downfall of their friendship, and she refused to let him slip from her life.

Josie reached for Reese and she could have sworn she heard him mutter something like "finally," but she wasn't positive. Her heart beat too fast, the thumping rhythm drowning out anything else.

All at once his hands were on her, his mouth covered hers, and he cupped her backside, lifting her against his firm body.

Every thought vanished as she let the overwhelming sensation of passion consume her. An unfamiliar feeling overcame her and all she could think was that this felt too right to be considered wrong.

Reese turned and moved them through the room, never taking his lips from hers. Josie laced her fingers behind his neck and held on as anticipation built and her body ached for so much more.

She tilted and landed softly on the comforter as Reese came down to rest on her. The weight of his body pressed her deeper into his warm bed.

The way he settled between her thighs had Josie tipping her hips, silently begging him for more. Reese's lips left hers and roamed over her jaw and down the column of her throat. She arched her back, granting him access to anything and everything he wanted.

His weight lifted off her as he eased his way down her body. Strong hands tugged at her chemise and Josie reached down to help him. She shimmied the silk up and over her head, tossing it aside without a care, leaving her only in her lace panties.

Reese came up to his knees, and in the glow of the moonlight, she didn't miss the way his heavy gaze raked over her body like this was the very first time seeing her.

He'd seen her plenty—in all kinds of outfits, in a bikini—but never like this and never so intimately. She wanted to freeze this second, to remember his look forever. She'd never felt sexier or more beautiful than right now.

Josie lifted her knees and came up onto her elbows. She wanted him to touch her with more than his stare. She needed skin to skin, and she was done waiting.

In a flurry of movements, she worked off her panties and assisted him in taking off his boxer briefs. Reese slid off the bed for a moment and procured protection before coming back to her.

This was really happening.

Josie should have been worried, but all she could think of was how much she wanted him to join their bodies, to make them one. Nothing felt weird or awkward, even though this was Reese.

Actually, she was surprised how perfect it felt.

He braced his hands on either side of her head and leaned down to glide his lips over hers.

"Be sure," he murmured.

Josie wrapped her arms and legs around him,

guiding him to exactly where she wanted him. The second he slid into her, Josie's body bowed as she cried out. Her fingertips dug into his shoulders and Reese immediately set a rhythm that did glorious things to her.

With his strong grip on her hips, Reese eased up and stared down at her while he made love to her.

No. They weren't making love.

This was sex. She hadn't planned for anything more.

"Get out of your head," he told her. "Stay with me."

He eased back down, slowed his pace and smoothed her hair away from her face. She didn't know how he always knew what she was thinking. He was just amazing like that.

Speaking of amazing, the way he moved his body over hers, glided his lips across her skin, had her body climbing higher. Josie gripped his hair as he covered her mouth with his. Her ankles locked even tighter as her climax hit.

He didn't release her lips as he swallowed her moans. Her knees pressed against his waist as every possible emotion overcame her. The intense pleasure and utter serenity completely took over. Josie lost herself in the moment, the man.

Nothing could ever compare to this right here.

Before she could come down from her high, Reese pulled his lips from hers, pumped even harder, and she watched as his jaw clenched. Those bright blue eyes locked onto hers as his release rolled through him.

Josie had never seen a sexier sight.

This was the only side to Reese she had never seen, and she honestly hadn't known she could get turned on so much even after her body had stopped trembling.

But seeing him come undone, well, Josie figured she'd be staying the night in this bed because she wasn't finished here.

Reese eased back down, shifting to the side and gathering her in against his side.

"Stay," he whispered.

Again, such a simple word that held so much meaning, so much promise.

Josie turned, tipping her head up to his as she raked a finger across his jawline. "I'm just getting started," she whispered back.

Nine

"Who were you referring to when you said you couldn't be her?"

Reese didn't mean to break the silence with that question, but he'd been wondering for some time now and obviously Josie wasn't going to be forthcoming with the information.

Just in the past two days he'd discovered there was much more to her than he'd ever realized. Clearly, she'd held this secret, but she'd also been hiding a passion that matched his, which he hadn't even considered.

Knowing they were compatible in more ways than just as friends blew his mind.

Having Josie in his bed had been more than he'd ever imagined…and he had a hell of an imagination where she was concerned. But realizing they were so damn compatible was just another confirmation that a physical relationship had been worth the risk.

The silence stretched between them as she sat on the edge of the bed with her bare back to him. The sun hadn't even come up yet and she was trying to leave. She'd spent the night here, they'd gotten little sleep, and they had to get ready to go to this interview at his restaurant and attempt to fake an engagement.

Reese would rather stay in this bed and figure out what was really going on between them, to know what she was thinking. Physically, she was here, but he wasn't sure she was with him mentally.

"What do you mean?" she asked, glancing over her shoulder.

That long, silky black hair fell down her back and he had the strongest urge to reach up and feel those strands slide between his fingertips.

"In your closet the other day," he reminded her. "The one with the leak. Who were you referring to when you said you couldn't be like her?"

Her eyes darted down, but even from her silhouette, he could see the sadness in her expression. Reese eased closer, but didn't touch her. He still didn't know where they'd landed in this postcoital moment, and he didn't want to make things awkward. He wanted her to feel comfortable enough to answer his question.

"My mother," she murmured. "I don't remember much about her, but I do remember her always wearing bright colors. She loved blues and reds. She always had on red lipstick, too."

Reese had never met Josie's mother, and actually hadn't seen many pictures of her, either. But he did recall seeing one photo, years ago, and Josie looked exactly like her mother. The long, dark hair, the doe eyes, the petite frame and the flawless, light brown skin tone.

"I remember Dad saying that when he first met mom during his travels to the Philippines, when he first joined the army, he fell in love with her on the spot. He loved how bold and vibrant she was. She challenged him and made him work for her affection. They were so in love."

Reese wanted to erase that sorrow from her tone, but he wasn't sorry that he'd asked. This was a portion of Josie that she'd kept locked away from him. They'd been friends for so many years, yet he'd never heard her talk of her mother this way and he sure as hell hadn't had a clue that she'd kept a shrine to her in her closet in the form of unworn clothes.

"Were those clothes hers?" he asked.

"No." Josie came to her feet and slid back into her chemise before settling back down and turning to face him. "I buy them thinking I'll take the plunge one day and just step out in something bold like she always did. But I'm not her. I'm boring, predictable and more comfortable in black. Besides, that's how my readers know me—classic black. Any photo I'm in or any event I attend, I'm always in black. It's my signature look now."

She attempted a soft smile, but that sadness still remained in her eyes. Had she always had that underlying emotion? Did he just take for granted that she was okay with how her life had turned out? He couldn't imagine losing his mother, but he doubted Josie would ever feel whole with that void in her life.

He was still trying to figure out how he felt regarding the fact that he was adopted. Now he had three parents and his world was all over the place. Even so, this was nothing like what Josie had gone through.

"You can wear whatever you want whenever you want," he informed her. "Be yourself. If that's a bright red dress, then do it."

She gave him a sideways glare, that typical Josie look when he suggested something she thought was a completely moronic idea.

"I'm serious," he urged. "There's no dress police. Maybe that could be your next article. How to revamp yourself—or some clever title you'd come up with."

Josie laughed and relief washed over him. He always wanted to hear her laugh, to see her wide smile and know she was happy.

"I wouldn't use something so trite as the word *revamp* in my title. I'm beyond college days when I was too tired to come up with something catchy."

She came to her feet again and smoothed her hair back from her face with a sigh. "Besides, I'm not getting the equivalent of an adult makeover, so this plan is irrelevant. I'm fine with who I am, I just sometimes wonder what it would be like. That's all."

Reese sat up in bed, the sheet pooled around his waist. He kept his eyes on that body he'd worshipped nearly all night. He wanted to know if she'd join him again tonight, because one night wasn't nearly enough, but he wanted to leave that next step up to her. He wasn't ready for a long-term commitment and he didn't want her to misunderstand what was happening here. It was up to her to continue what they'd started. She'd come to him once before…he had to believe she would again.

"I'm going to get ready," she told him. "If we leave early, we can swing by Rise and Grind. I haven't had an iced mocha latte in forever."

"You had one last week. I picked it up for you and brought it to your house and even delivered it into your home office."

Her brows drew in as if she were trying to remember, but then she shrugged. "Well, a week is too long."

Reese shoved the covers aside and rose. Josie's eyes immediately landed on his bare body and then darted away.

"You're not going to act embarrassed, are you?" he asked, purposely not grabbing his clothes.

"No, no." She glanced anywhere but at him. "Nothing to be embarrassed about, right? We're both adults and last night was…it was…"

Reese bit the inside of his cheek to keep from laughing at her stammering and her focus darting all around the room like she was trying to find something to land on other than him or their night together.

He rounded the bed and came up behind her. Not touching her took a considerable amount of willpower, though.

"No regrets," he told her.

Josie jumped, clearly unaware he'd moved closer.

"I don't have regrets," she stated, still without looking at him. "I have concerns."

Might as well be the same thing, but he wanted to alleviate any worries.

"Nothing we did was wrong," he told her, taking her shoulders and turning her to face him. "You know that, right?"

Her eyes caught his as she nodded. "I just don't want things to change."

"How would they change? We both had a great

time, we both enjoyed it…if your moaning and panting my name were any indicators."

She rolled her eyes and smacked his bare chest, which was the exact response he wanted. He needed to lighten the mood so she didn't feel like this was anything more than what it was…sex between friends. He didn't want her worried or afraid that they couldn't still be the best of friends.

They were both on unfamiliar ground here. And he wasn't sure how the hell to even start setting boundaries. All he knew was that he wanted her on a level he'd never wanted anyone before…the rest could sort itself out later.

"We won't start comparing notes," she said with a smile. "You did your fair share of that sexy clenched-jaw thing so I know you had a good time."

"Sexy jaw thing?" he asked. He had no idea what that meant, but he'd had a good time. He decided to zero in on the fact that she'd called him sexy.

Maybe they would be right back in his bed tonight.

"Your ego needs no help from me," she told him as she took a step back. "And I need to get ready. Coffee is on you this morning."

She sashayed out, but not before tossing him another grin that punched him with a heavy dose of lust. He had no idea how this interview would go or what they'd be expected to do in the photo shoot, but none of that mattered.

Reese was already counting down the time until they came back here, and he could get to know more of that sweet body of hers.

"And if you could slide the back of your finger-tips down her cheek," the photographer suggested.

Josie stilled, her palms flat against Reese's chest. He had one arm wrapped around her waist and had her flush against his body, while he used the other hand to obey the photographer's commands.

"Now lock eyes," the photographer added. "Like you're dying to kiss, but you can't."

Well, at least that part wasn't fake. With Reese this close and her hormones still in overdrive from last night, she desperately wanted to feel his lips on hers…sans an audience.

Was that normal? Should she want to strip down her best friend? She wasn't even sure what to call this newfound relationship they'd created, but she also knew if she read too much into it, she'd drive herself mad.

Maybe she just needed to create a new box, one without a label but still a nice, neat area to keep these emotions in for now—until she knew what to do with them.

"A little closer," the photographer stated as she snapped away.

She moved in closer and Josie tried not to break

eye contact with Reese, but the lights and the people standing around watching were a bit unnerving.

They'd set up just inside the stunning entryway of Conrad's. With the serene waterfall wall, the suspended glass bulbs showcasing pale greenery, the place seemed simple, yet classy, and perfect for a photo where the photographer wanted to focus on the couple.

"Breathe," Reese whispered.

Her eyes held his and that desire staring back at her had her heart beating even faster. Having sex and being in the dark was one thing, but pretending to be in love with lights and cameras all around was definitely another.

Melissa stood off to the side, smiling like a mother of the bride. Guilt settled deep. All of this had started simply because she wanted her ex to move on.

One failed marriage was embarrassing enough. She didn't want to be known for another unsuccessful relationship. Perhaps she and Reese would fool everyone with these photos of a couple in love and then once they announced they were better off as friends, people would see them in public together, and everything would go back to normal.

She hoped.

"Oh, wait a minute."

Josie jerked away from Reese when her editor interrupted the clicking of the camera.

"Where's her ring?" Melissa asked. "We can't do photo shoot about the engagement without the ring."

Josie froze. The ring? Damn it, she hadn't thought that far ahead. Reese had joked about it, but that had just been him trying to annoy her in that playful way of his. They weren't actually going ring shopping. Good grief, that would be absurd, but she couldn't think of a lie right off the top of her head.

Her eyes darted back to Reese's, who was reaching into his pocket.

"Right here," he stated, producing a ruby set in a diamond band. "I cleaned it for her this morning and we were in a rush to get here, so I slipped it into my pocket."

Josie's attention volleyed between Reese's sexy grin and that ring she'd never seen before in her life. Was he serious? How in the hell did he just procure a ring—a rather impressive, expensive-looking ring—out of his pants pocket? Even Reese wasn't that powerful...was he? How had he made this happen and why hadn't he clued her in on it?

"Here you go, babe."

Reese lifted her left hand and slid the ring into place and the damn thing actually fit like it was made for her. Had he known her ring size, too?

"Let me see," exclaimed her editor.

Josie was busy examining the rock herself because this was seriously a piece of art. When her editor grabbed her hand and squealed, Josie couldn't help but laugh. She glanced back to Reese, who merely winked, as if he'd had everything under control from the start.

Again, the man took care of all the details and never acted like he was put out or tired. How did he do all of that without a planner, a spreadsheet, a personal assistant?

Okay, he had assistants, but Reese was also very hands-on. There was no way he'd send an assistant to get an engagement ring, not even a fake one.

"You two are so lucky," Melissa stated, glancing between Josie and Reese. "Okay, get back to the shoot. I just had to see what he chose and it's absolutely perfect."

Josie glanced around at the crew staring and waiting on them to continue. "Um, could Reese and I have two minutes?"

Everyone nodded and Josie grabbed Reese's hand and pulled him toward the back of the open room. There wasn't much privacy to be had, but she had to use what she could.

She turned so that Reese's broad frame blocked her from the rest of the audience.

"Where did you get this?" she whispered between gritted teeth.

Reese smiled. "I couldn't let my fiancée be without a ring. That wouldn't say much about our love, now would it?"

She narrowed her eyes at his sarcasm.

Of course he only smiled and replied, "I bought it."

He bought it. Like he'd just gone out and gotten a pair of shoes or a new cell phone. She didn't even want to know what this ring cost.

"Can you return it?"

Reese's brows drew in. "Return it? Why?"

She couldn't say much with their current lack of privacy, so she merely widened her eyes and tipped her head, knowing he could practically read her mind most times.

"It's yours, Jo. Think of it as a birthday present if that makes you feel better."

That soft tone of his had her heart melting and she firmly told her heart not to get involved. Whatever this was going on with them had to be structured or the entire faux engagement would explode in her face, taking her heart in the process.

"I'm sorry, but we still have to get to the interview," Melissa chimed in. "We do have deadlines, you know."

Yeah, Josie was well aware of deadlines—when it came to work *and* Reese.

Less than two weeks now.

Josie glanced down to the ring on her finger, the symbol of so much more than what was actually going on. There was another layer of guilt because each day that went by, she found herself deeper into this lie.

The deep red stone stared back at her and she

wondered what on earth made him choose one so bold instead of a traditional diamond. She also wondered what the hell she'd do with an engagement ring once the engagement ended.

Reese lifted her hand and kissed the spot just above the ring as his eyes remained locked onto hers.

"Ready?" he asked.

Was she ready? She didn't know how to answer that because she had a feeling he wasn't talking about the pictures.

The ring weighed heavy on her hand as they went back to the crew. This farce was almost over. She only had to hang on until after the Manhattan opening and then they could go back to the way things were before…if that was even possible.

Ten

Reese had never been more relieved than when that interview was over. There were some questions he and Josie definitely had to fudge, but they'd sounded believable and that's all that mattered.

And when he'd asked her to take the rest of the day off, he'd never thought she'd actually do it. Yet here they were, leaving her house after she wanted to pick up a few things and check on the progress of the work.

Reese's crew said it would be at least another week because they'd run into some other issues they were fixing while there. Fine by Reese. He was in no hurry to get her out of his bed.

"I assume you're taking me somewhere for my birthday and it has something to do with the beach."

They both loved being outside whenever possible. Their schedules were so demanding, and nothing relaxed them quite like the gentle waves and the calming winds off the ocean.

Reese pulled out of her drive and said nothing. He wanted this evening to be all about her and he wanted her to relax without worrying about the fake engagement, the article, the renovations on her house…nothing.

He also needed a break from his thoughts and issues. Josie was always the answer when he needed some space from reality.

"I'm not telling you what the surprise is," he stated. "We already went over that."

"That was yesterday. I'm going to find out soon anyway."

"Then that's when you'll know and not a minute before."

He didn't even care that she pouted and turned her attention out the window. He'd planned a perfect birthday evening and she would love it.

"You're coming to the opening with me next weekend, right?" he asked as he turned down his private road.

"I wouldn't miss it."

"I want you to cover it, if you don't mind multitasking as my date and my journalist."

Now she glanced toward him with a smile on her face. How did her smile turn him on? It was such a simple gesture, yet packed such a lustful punch. Maybe that's why he always wanted to make her smile.

"I am quite capable of doing both," she informed him. "So my surprise is at your house?"

Laughing, Reese pulled up and waited for his gate to open. "Something like that."

She remained silent as he parked and gathered her things.

"Follow me," he ordered as he followed the path around the back of the house, leading toward his dock.

"Oh, a ride on the yacht," she exclaimed. "Fun. It's a beautiful afternoon."

A perfect day for relaxing…and maybe more. He'd planned this birthday surprise well before last night, so now he couldn't help but wonder if they'd pick back up where they'd left off.

Reese assisted her down the dock and onto the yacht. His chef stood at the entrance to the cabin and nodded as they stepped on board. Frisco wasn't just his chef, though that was his main position and what he'd been hired for, but the man did absolutely everything Reese asked and typically a little more. He was invaluable.

"Good afternoon, Reese. Miss Coleman."

"Thanks for setting everything up, Frisco." Reese

slapped the man on the back. "That will be all. Take the rest of the day off."

"Thank you, sir."

Once Frisco left them, Reese gestured for Josie to step on into the cabin.

"Go change," he urged. "I'll get things ready to go."

"Don't you want to change, too?"

He took a step closer, but didn't reach for her. "Is that an invitation?"

Her eyes clouded with desire, a look that had been new to him only days ago, but now he knew it all too well. Even though they'd only spent one night together, he wanted so much more. One night was not nearly enough time to explore all things Josie.

"Isn't that why you sent Frisco away?" she asked, quirking a brow.

"I sent him away because I want to spend your birthday with you, under the sun and then the stars, out on the water, without anyone around. He's done all I needed him to do."

Her eyes raked down him in a way that he hadn't experienced before. Reese liked this side of Josie and had to admit his ego swelled a little—okay, more than a little—knowing he had a hand in drawing out her passion.

"Maybe I need help changing into my suit," she purred as she reached for the hem of her black pencil dress.

She pulled it up and over her head, tossing the garment to the side. Josie stood before him in only a matching black silky bra-and-pantie set and those little black heels. With all of that dark hair pulled back, he wanted to yank the pins out and mess it all up.

"You surprise me," he told her. "That's not something I ever thought I'd say with you."

Josie shrugged. "I may like to plan everything, but I also know what I want."

Arousal slammed into him.

"And what's that?" he asked.

With her eyes firmly set on his, she reached for the snap of his dress pants. "More of last night."

Reese shoved her hands away and wrapped his arms around her waist, hauling her up against his chest as he claimed her mouth. He needed no further permission to take what she so freely offered.

Josie locked her ankles behind his back as Reese crossed the living quarters. The accent table on his way stopped him, though. He wasn't going to make it to the bedroom, not with the way Josie was clawing at his shirt.

She jerked his shirt up as he dropped his pants and boxer briefs to the floor. Josie laughed as he attempted to toe off his shoes and kick his clothes aside. A few random strands of her hair had fallen across her face, but he wanted her even more out of control.

Reese reached behind her and released the fastener holding her hair up. The silky strands instantly fell around her shoulders and her laugh quickly sobered as she stared up at him.

He gripped her hips and scooted her closer to the edge of the table. When he slid a finger inside her panties to pull them aside, she curled her fingers around his shoulders.

"Protection?" she asked.

He glanced toward the bedroom where he'd been heading. "In there," he nodded.

She bit down on her lip and jerked her hips against his hand. "I trust you. I just had a checkup and I'm on birth control."

Reese swallowed. Never in his life had he gone without a condom, and knowing he had the okay to do so with Josie was a hell of an unexpected turn-on.

"I'm clean," he assured her. "I'd never do anything to hurt you."

She locked her gaze with his and nodded, giving him the silent affirmation to go ahead.

Holding the thin material aside, Reese slid into her, earning him another of her slow, sultry moans.

He gritted his teeth, taking just a fraction of a moment to relish the fact that no barriers stood between them. This was a first for him.

But the urge and the overwhelming need to have her took hold again and he couldn't remain still.

Josie lifted her pelvis against his, urging him on, and Reese was more than ready to comply.

Josie lifted her knees against his sides, wrapped her arms around his neck and covered his mouth. He might physically be in the dominant position, but she held all the power. He was utterly useless when it came to her, and she could do anything she wanted.

There was frantic need coming off her in waves, a feeling he couldn't quite identify, but now was not the time to analyze her every thought or motive. All he wanted was more of this reckless, unrestrained Josie.

Reese reached around and flicked open her bra. Never removing his lips from hers, he fumbled enough to get the bra off and away so he could claim handfuls of her breasts. He wanted all of her, as much as she would give, and he was so damn glad he didn't have to hide his desire anymore.

"Reese," she murmured against his lips.

Her body quickened and he slid a hand between them to touch her at her most sensitive spot, knowing it would drive her over the edge.

Her gasp against his mouth and the way her entire body tightened had him pumping even faster, working toward his own release. Josie cried out and dropped her head to that crook in his neck. Reese used his free hand to press against the small of her back, making them even more flush for the best possible experience.

That's when euphoria took over and his body started trembling. Josie's warm breath hit the side of his neck, only adding to the shivers consuming him.

Her fingers slid through his hair as she placed a kiss on his heated skin.

Reese blew out a slow breath when his body calmed. It took another minute for him to regain the strength to pull away, but he only eased back slightly to look down at her.

"Still need help with that suit?" he asked.

"I think I need some water," she laughed. "And maybe food if that's any indication of how my birthday surprise is going to go."

Reese smiled. "That's not exactly what I had planned for your birthday, so we're both surprised."

Reese took a step back and helped her from the table. He still wore his shirt and nothing else, while she still had on her panties, which were now very askew.

Fast, frantic sex had never crossed his mind when it came to Josie. He'd always thought he'd take his time and explore every inch of her. He hadn't rushed last night, but he still hadn't taken the time he wanted. And just now? Yeah, that was the fastest sex on his record.

But he wasn't sorry.

Josie had set the pace; she had wanted him here and now. Who was he to deny her…and on her birthday no less?

Reese unbuttoned his shirt and went to pick up his other clothes strewn over the floor.

Josie slid out of her panties and gathered her things, throwing him a smile over her shoulder as she headed toward the suite.

Reese barely got to enjoy the bare view when his cell chimed in the pocket of his pants. He shuffled the pieces in his hand until he could find the phone. Clutching everything under his arm, he glanced to the screen and contemplated letting it go to voice mail. He really didn't want any interruptions, but his parents couldn't just be ignored.

And he was going to have to tell them what he'd found. They were going to be at his new opening, but he needed to talk to them before that. His big night in Manhattan certainly wasn't the time to tell them he was aware of the adoption and knew who his biological father was.

With a sigh, he slid his finger over the screen.

"Hey," he answered. "Still enjoying the mountains?"

"Hi, sweetheart," his mother answered in that smiling tone she had. "We are actually heading back home. We're on our way to the airport now."

"Home?" he questioned. "I thought you were only coming to New York next weekend. Are you guys okay?"

"We're fine," she assured him. "You know how

your dad is. He just feels useless if he's not doing something productive."

"He retired," Reese reminded her. "He's supposed to be useless right now, relaxing in some amazing location that will give you guys all the drinks and massages you want."

His mother laughed. "Sounds good to me, but I think he misses you. I mean, I do, too, but he worries you're taking on too much and he just wants to support you and be there if you need advice."

Reese pinched the bridge of his nose and closed his eyes. "I've been doing this my whole life. I've got it covered."

"I tried to tell him that, but you have to remember he doesn't know what to do with his days right now. Just, maybe give him a little piddly job or, I don't know, ask his opinion on something?"

There were a million things involved in running a successful chain of upscale restaurants, and that was before adding in a brand-new opening. Reese could no doubt find something for his father.

Josie came back through wearing a one-piece black bathing suit that shouldn't have his body revving up again, but...well, it did.

"I'll see what I can do," Reese told his mother without taking his eyes off Josie. "Could you and Dad come to the house tomorrow?"

"I'm sure we can. Everything all right?"

Reese tore his eyes from Josie. He hadn't meant

to just blurt out that he needed to see them, but now that he had, he'd follow through. As uncomfortable as this conversation was going to be, he wanted the truth.

"I'm fine," he assured her. "I just have something I don't want to discuss over the phone."

"Well, I'm intrigued. We'll be there around one if that works for you."

"I'll have Frisco prepare lunch. Have a safe flight. Love you, Mom."

He hung up and clutched his cell at his side. Should he just leave this letter alone? He and his parents had a great relationship; there was no reason to pull all of this past out in the open.

But he had two half brothers that he wanted to pursue a relationship with and he had to be honest with his parents about the events that had happened since they'd been gone.

"Are you skinny-dipping or putting on trunks?"

Josie's question pulled him back to the moment. He glanced toward the glass doors overlooking the sparkling ocean and back to the woman who expected him to follow through on this birthday celebration.

She deserved it all, and he wasn't going to let this unexpected bomb in his personal life affect her day.

"Do you have a preference?" he asked with a wink.

She merely laughed and shook her head. "You sounded serious with your mom. If this fake engagement is getting to be too much, you can go ahead and tell her the truth."

"What? No, that's not it." He sat his clothes down on the curved sofa and pulled on his boxer briefs. "I just have something to discuss with them that I don't want to wait on since they're coming home early."

Josie tipped her head, her ponytail sliding over one shoulder. "Is it the restaurant opening? You haven't acted like you're worried about it."

"I'm not," he assured her truthfully. "My team is on it and I was just up there. I know that night will be perfect."

Her brows drew in. "Oh, I didn't know there was something else bothering you. I just assume if something is wrong that you know I'm always here to listen."

Well, now he felt like a jerk.

Reese stepped forward, wanting to console her, but selfishly wanting his hands back on her body. He found the more he was with her, the more difficult it was to keep his distance…especially now that he knew exactly how she felt and how she trembled beneath his touch.

"I do tell you everything," he assured her. "You're my best friend, Jo. Let's just enjoy your day and talk tomorrow. Deal?"

He really needed to talk to his parents before he opened up to her. He owed them that much, giving them the courtesy of explaining their side and listening to what they had to say.

Josie reached up and patted his cheek. "Ignore me. You don't owe me an explanation. I just want you to know I'm here anytime."

His settled his hands on the dip in her waist and pulled her closer. "I'm well aware you're here. But today, let me pamper you. Now go out and lounge on the sundeck. I'll get changed and we'll take off. I'll join you in a bit."

She looked like she wanted to say more, but she nodded and stepped away. When she hit the steps leading up, she turned back.

"Hurry. I need someone to rub sunscreen on my back."

That was an invitation he couldn't ignore. For now, he was just going to focus on Josie. He wasn't going to think about the father he'd never met, telling his parents he knew the truth and he certainly wasn't going to think about the way the words *best friends* sounded wrong when he'd said them because they were more.

He just had to figure out how the hell to keep both of them from getting hurt when this all went back to platonic, because after he had his opening in Manhattan when they needed to be seen arm in arm, they would have to face reality.

And the reality was...all of this was temporary.

Eleven

Josie barely recognized herself. First, she'd ditched work, then she'd lain around the yacht letting Reese ply her with mai tais, and now she was enjoying a candlelight dinner on the deck with the full moon shining down on them.

She had to admit this birthday was turning out to be pretty awesome.

"You're going to spoil me," she told him as she reached for her wineglass.

Reese sat his napkin on the table and leaned back in his chair. "It's your birthday. I'm supposed to spoil you."

Josie didn't mean just today or in this moment.

She meant in general. Reese had always been the one to comfort her, to make sure she was happy, to have her back at all times.

Hence the faux engagement.

But the undercurrent in this relationship had shifted and she was discovering that it was difficult to find her footing. She should feel guilty for wanting more sex, for enjoying it as much as she was, because there would come a time when they had to revert back to being just friends. They couldn't go on this way forever. At some point, Reese might want to find someone and settle down and have a family. That's how he was raised; that's all he knew—family and business.

Oh, she knew he dated and jet-setted around with multiple women, but none of those relationships lasted and he'd never claimed to have been in love before. He'd also never acted like he wanted to marry anytime soon, which had made that engagement months ago all the more shocking, but Josie knew the day would come. Reese's genetic makeup was that of a family man, of heritage and legacy. Those were just traits ingrained in him.

She, on the other hand, knew nothing of that type of commitment or long-term bond and the idea terrified her. Her family had been ripped apart, and then the emotional walls went up. Reese had been the only one she'd firmly clung to.

She was proud of herself, though. She'd stepped out of her comfort zone and been bold enough to take what she wanted. But how did she go back to what she'd been once everything was done? When they didn't need to show their faces to the public and they could just be Reese and Josie, best friends? Was that even possible?

So, sex was good. It was great, in fact. Josie figured she'd just enjoy herself, enjoy this bit of freedom she'd never allowed herself to have, and hope nobody got hurt in the end because she still needed that rock her best friend provided. She always had.

Josie glanced down to the ring on her finger and couldn't deny how much she loved the sparkling piece. The oval ruby surrounded by twinkling diamonds. She'd never given an engagement ring much thought before.

"Looks good on you."

She turned her attention to Reese, who nodded toward her hand. "I knew a ruby would look good on you."

"You were just dying to get some color on me," she laughed. "It's beautiful, but you know I can't keep this."

"Sure you can. I told you, consider it your birthday gift, but for now the public can believe it's your engagement ring."

"Reese—"

He reached across the table and grabbed her hand, stroking his thumb over the stone. "A friend can't buy another friend a nice birthday gift?"

She didn't know why every time he threw out the word *friend* she felt a little...off. Josie couldn't quite find the right word for how the word made her feel, but it certainly wasn't settled.

She hated disruption in her life. She'd grown up with a very regimented, standoffish father, and all of that rearing had carried over into her adult life. Everything had changed after her mother passed because, looking back, Josie realized that it was her mother who had been doting and loving, while her father demanded structure and obedience.

Josie still craved that safe zone, the comfort of knowing every aspect of her life was in the proper place.

"I got you something else," he said, hopping up from the table.

"I don't need anything else," she laughed. "The cruise, the dinner, the ring. I'm good, Reese."

He smiled down at her. "Trust me, this was not expensive, but I couldn't resist."

Now she was intrigued. She waited while he stepped down into the cabin and then came back holding a small, narrow box that was so small there was no bow. Just simple wrapping.

"It's really not much," he repeated, handing the gift over. "But I hope you'll put it to good use."

She took the gift, but kept her eyes on him. "It's too small to be a sex toy."

Reese laughed. "I'm all the sex toy you need right now."

Right now.

Josie let the words wash over her. She tried to brush them aside, but they wiggled their way right past the giddiness that consumed her and hit her heart. The simple term took hold, threatening to penetrate and cause pain.

She refused to let their current situation hurt her or damage their friendship.

Ignoring thoughts of the future, Josie tore the paper and discovered her present.

"A tube of red lipstick?"

She glanced up to Reese, who stood there smiling.

"I figure if you're not comfortable wearing the clothes, maybe we could ease you into the color."

She stared at the name brand and was actually impressed he'd known what to purchase. "I'm not sure bright red lips would be easing into wearing color."

"Just try it," he told her. "Don't let fear win, Jo. That's all this is. Fear. It's a tube of lipstick. I'm not asking you to skydive."

Josie took the cosmetic from the box and slid the lid off. Turning the base, she stared at the vibrant shade and wondered how the hell she could pull that off. Her makeup regimen consisted of mascara, black of course, and sometimes a sheer gloss if she wanted to be extra.

"Listen," he told her as he pulled his chair around the table and next to hers. He grabbed her hands and set the tube on the table. "I'm not trying to make you into someone you're not. I'm not trying to make you uncomfortable, but you have all of this inside of you. If you want to channel your mother or pay tribute to her in some way, then do it. Do it for you, and who gives a damn what other people think."

She stared into those bright blue eyes and wondered how she'd never gotten lost in them before. How had she never noticed just how remarkable Reese was? Not just to look at, because she'd known for years how hot he was, but he was her friend… right? She shouldn't have had lustful thoughts.

Yet now she did.

They'd been intimate a handful of times and she already had enough fantasies to last a lifetime.

Beyond his looks, though, there was that heart of gold. He dominated everything around him, but not in an asshole kind of way. Yes, he demanded respect, but his loyal circle of friends and employees loved him and would do anything for him. That was the sign of a true leader.

"Why did we never date when we were younger?" she asked before she could stop herself, because they weren't even dating now.

His brows drew in as he released her hands and sat back in his chair. "I asked you out."

Confused, Josie racked her brain, but drew a blank. "You did? When?"

"In college," he told her as if she should remember. "I was helping you move from the dorm into your first apartment and I asked you out."

She recalled when he'd helped her. They thought they'd never get her hand-me-down couch up that flight of stairs to the second floor. They'd laughed, argued, shared a horrible pizza for dinner.

Oh yeah. That's when he'd asked her.

"I thought you were joking," she finally stated, but caught the sober look on his face. "You were serious?"

Reese didn't smile. He didn't make a move as he continued to stare back at her. "I'd never been more serious."

Oh. Well.

What did she do with that information?

She couldn't exactly go back in time, but if she could, would she have said yes? Josie had never thought of Reese as more than a friend until recently, but the word *more* was such a blanket term. It could be applied to anything.

She didn't know how to reply to his statement, but he had clearly thought about this over the years because he hadn't forgotten the moment. Obviously, there had been a bigger impact on him than her.

What exactly did that mean? Surely he didn't want to take this beyond best friend territory…did he?

"Reese, I—"

He leaned forward and cut her words off with a kiss. She melted into his powerful touch, completely forgetting anything she needed to say.

"No more talking," he murmured against her lips. "I want you wearing nothing but that ring and the moonlight."

Shivers raced through her at his sexy command. Anything they needed to discuss or work out with this relationship could be done later, because Reese was stripping her clothes off and she had a feeling she was about to get another birthday present.

"I discovered I'm adopted."

Josie's gasp over the warm night air seemed to echo.

It was well past midnight, so technically her birthday was over. They were on their way back to his place, fully dressed, and he found he couldn't keep the news from her any longer. The only people who knew that he knew the truth were strangers. Reese needed her advice and her shoulder to lean on. That was the main thing he valued about their relationship. Even when he was trying to be strong, to put up a front of steel, he could let his guard down around her and she never criticized or judged him.

He'd wanted to tell his parents first. He really thought he owed them that. But the other part of him needed Josie's advice on how to handle such a delicate situation. There was nobody he trusted more with this secret.

"Adopted?" she repeated. "Reese, how... I mean, who told you? Are you sure?"

He guided the yacht toward his dock. In the distance, his three-story beachfront home lit up the shoreline. He always loved this time of night when the water was calm and quiet. He needed a stillness in however he could manage to gain one, in order to keep his sanity.

"I'm pretty certain," he told her, still keeping his eye on the dock. "I also found out I have two half brothers in Green Valley, Tennessee."

"That was the reason for your trip."

He nodded as he felt her come up beside him. The wind whipped her hair, sending strands drifting over his bare arm.

"Who are your birth parents?" she asked.

Reese shrugged. "I received a letter from a woman who I found out was my half brother's mom. She was dying and before she passed, she sent three letters. Even her son didn't know who his father was growing up, but she wanted to clear the air, I guess. Anyway, I don't know about my birth mother, but my biological father is Rusty Lockwood."

"Lockwood," she murmured. "As in, Lockwood Lightning?"

"Yeah."

"Wow." Josie laid her delicate hand on his arm for support. "Have you met him?"

Reese slowed the engine as he neared the dock. "No, but I've not heard pleasant things about him and in my own research, I've read some disturbing news. He's certainly no comparison to Martin Conrad."

The gentle squeeze from her touch had a bit of his anxiety sliding away.

"Nobody is Martin Conrad," she agreed. "Do your parents know you found this out?"

"No. That's what I want to talk to them about tomorrow."

He still didn't know how to approach the topic other than just showing them the letter and giving them a chance to explain.

"Do you…um, do you need me there?" she asked, her tone low, uncertain. "I mean, I don't want to step over the line and make you uncomfortable, but if you need someone—"

Reese reached up and slid his hand over hers as he glanced her way for a brief moment. "I want you there."

She seemed to exhale a breath and her body relaxed against his. "I don't even know what to say, but I'll do whatever I can for you."

He knew she would. He knew no matter what decision he made, she would stand by him.

"I'm going to Green Valley in a few days." He

steered the ship expertly between the docks. "I'd like you to come with me if you can get away."

"I'll make the time, and I can always work on the road," she told him. "Or are we taking the jet?"

"It's going to be a quick trip," he stated, killing the engine. "We'll fly to save time."

She nodded and smiled. "Tell me when to be ready and I'll be there."

Once the yacht was secure and he'd assisted her off the dock, Reese blocked her path to head back to the house. He framed her face with his hands and leaned closer.

"You said I would spoil you, but I think it's the other way around," he murmured against her mouth. "Maybe I'm the one getting spoiled because I don't deserve all I want to take from you."

Reese wrapped his arms around her, pulling her against his chest and claiming her lips. He didn't want to talk, didn't want to think, didn't want to consider tomorrow or even the day after that. Right now, he wanted to take Jo back to his bedroom and show her just how much he ached for her.

Because their two weeks were slowly coming to an end, and he wasn't quite ready to let this physical relationship go. And maybe there was more, maybe there was something beyond the physical. Reese wasn't sure if he was getting the friendship bond confused with something more or not…he only prayed nobody got hurt in the end.

Twelve

"Darling, you look so happy."

Reese cringed when his mother wrapped her arms around him and then stepped back to examine him and Josie, who stood at his side.

"I cannot tell you how thrilled I am that the two of you are together," she went on. "I've known for years you were the one for my son."

Josie's eyes darted to his, but Reese merely smiled. He had bigger things to deal with right now than this fake engagement. He was about to crush the two people who loved him more than anything, who'd raised him like their own, who'd given him the life he lived today.

But they all deserved for the secrets to come out so they could move forward. He'd had time to deal with the truth. He knew his parents were good people and they likely had done what they thought was in his best interest.

"Can we at least get inside before you start smothering them?" Martin asked as he stepped into the foyer.

Reese stared at the man he'd always thought of as his father. He'd never given it much thought, but other than the fact that they were both tall with broad shoulders, there were no other similarities.

Laura reached for Josie and wrapped her arms around her, too. Reese hated the guilt that layered in with his anxiety. He'd never held on to this many secrets at one time in his life.

Between the engagement and the news about his biological father, Reese had to get something out in the open before he drove himself mad. The only saving grace in all of this was that Josie was finally in his bed, where he'd wanted her for longer than he cared to admit. Granted, now he didn't know how to take a step back with her into that friend territory. He honestly wasn't sure he wanted to, but they'd agreed that after his opening, they would make an announcement that they were better off as friends and call off this fake engagement.

What did it say about him that he wasn't ready for that announcement?

"Oh, my word, that ring is gorgeous," his mother declared, holding Josie's hand. "So unique and perfect."

"It's really beautiful," Josie stated, but Reese didn't miss the tightness in her tone. "Why don't you guys come on in? Frisco set up lunch out on the back deck."

Reese was thankful Josie took over and turned the attention away from the engagement, but that meant the next topic was another he didn't want to get into.

Lunch flew by with chatter and laughter, but Reese knew time was ticking and he'd have to just pull the letter from his pocket and share.

Josie's fingertip drew a pattern over the condensation on her water glass and he knew she was feeling all the nerves as well. He met her gaze and she offered him a reassuring smile.

"I'm glad to see you guys," Reese started. "But there's something I need to discuss."

His mother sat back in her seat and shifted her attention. "Yes, you have me intrigued. Is this about New York? You're not moving, are you?"

Reese shook his head. "I love it here and I'm fine with traveling wherever I need."

"Is something wrong, son?" his father asked, resting his elbows on the arms of the dining chair.

Reese reached into his pocket and pulled out the letter. He passed it to his father.

"I received this right after you were released from the hospital and I didn't want to bring it up," he added. "And then I wanted you guys to enjoy your trip, so I kept it to myself until I could sort things out."

Martin Conrad's eyes darted from Reese down to the folded letter. He opened the paper and started reading. It didn't take long for the color to drain from his face.

"Martin, what is it?"

His father remained silent as he finished reading, but ultimately he handed the letter across the table.

Reese's heart beat so hard, so fast, but he tried to remain calm. This was the best move in the long run; there would just be some painful hurdles to overcome.

Surprisingly, his mother didn't get upset. She squared her shoulders and placed the letter on the table, running her fingertip along the creases in a vain attempt to smooth it out.

Her dark brown eyes finally came up to his.

"I want you to know we did everything we could to make the best decision at the time," she told him. "We went through an agency, but the birth parents wanted to remain anonymous."

"That's when we decided not to tell you about the adoption because we had no more information to give," his father added. "You were our son from day one. Blood didn't matter."

No, it didn't. These were his parents and there had never been any doubt the lengths they would go to to make him happy and show their love.

"Do you hate us?" his mother finally asked. "I don't think I could stand it if you were upset with us. We just wanted to give you the best life."

Reese scooted his chair back and went around to his mom. "Never," he said, leaning down to wrap his arms around her. "I could never hate either of you. I just didn't want to keep this from you. I may always wonder why you didn't tell me before, but I respect that you have your reasons. I've never been a parent or in your shoes, so I can't judge."

"Well, now you have the birth father's name," his dad chimed in. "Have you reached out to him?"

Reese straightened, but kept his hand on his mother's shoulder. "No. I wouldn't have done that before talking to you. I did go to Green Valley, Tennessee, though. I've met with my half brothers. Nick Campbell and Sam Hawkins."

"Sam Hawkins," his dad murmured. "He's the son of Rusty Lockwood, too?"

Reese nodded. "And Nick is a major investor and renovator. He's opening a resort this fall in the Smoky Mountains. A project his late mom started."

"Sounds like all the boys turned out well," his mom said. "I don't know Rusty, other than through the Lockwood Lightning name."

Reese glanced to Josie, who had given her silent

support this entire time. He wasn't sure what all to get into regarding Rusty, but he knew he didn't want to think about it right now. He'd let the secret out; that had been his main goal.

"I plan on going back to Green Valley," Reese added. "Sam and Nick want to confront Rusty. All of us together."

His mother inhaled sharply and glanced up at him. He saw the fear in her eyes, but she remained strong. Two of the strongest women he'd ever known both had their eyes on him.

"I only want to meet him, maybe see if he knows the name of the woman who gave birth to me."

Now Laura Conrad's eyes did well up. The last thing he wanted was to cause her pain.

"I may not do anything with the information," he assured her. "I honestly don't know. All I know is this is still new to me and you guys have had years to process. I'm asking you to trust me to do what is right for me now."

Martin came to his feet and eased around the patio table. "Of course we trust you, son. You do what you think is best. We'll support you."

Reese nodded, worried if he said too much, emotions would clog his throat and overcome him. This delicate situation demanded control.

His father reached out and wrapped his arms around Reese. Patting his back, Reese took the embrace, this one meaning so much more than any in the past.

"Will you keep us posted on what you find?" his mother asked.

Reese turned back to face her and smiled. "Of course. Josie and I are going to Tennessee in a couple of days. I'm not sure how long we'll be there, so we may just go on to New York from there."

His mom came to her feet and opened her arms. He gathered her in, recognizing as always how petite yet resilient she was.

"I hope you find what you're looking for," she whispered. "I just don't want this to change us."

He eased back and held on to her slender shoulders. "You guys are my parents. Nothing can change that."

Over his mother's shoulder, Reese caught Josie swiping a tear. He didn't even think of the emotional impact this would have on her. Having a distant relationship with her father and no mother, this had to be difficult, seeing him with such a strong bond with both of his parents.

"I'll just leave you guys and start cleaning up." Josie eased her chair back and started reaching for the dishes. "I'll bring dessert in a few minutes."

"Don't clean up," Reese told her, but she was already stacking plates and carrying them away.

"You've got a good woman there," his father declared. "It's going to take a strong woman by your side to do the work we do."

Reese was well aware of that, but he hadn't thought of Josie by his side in that sense for the long term. They were friends…friends enjoying the hell out of each other and helping the other out during a difficult time.

Would his parents be disappointed when he told them he and Josie weren't actually going to get married? Maybe, but he would have to cross that bridge when they got to it.

And it wasn't like Josie was going anywhere, right? She would still be by his side as his friend. Her support was all he needed—the intimacy was just the fulfillment of something he'd been fantasizing about.

He had so many career goals to achieve before thinking of anything long-term with a woman. Besides, Josie never acted like she was ready for a commitment, either. So why was he stressing? Why was he feeling a heaviness, knowing the end of this farce was near?

"I was also thinking we could do a live timeline piece."

Josie had been taking diligent notes about the new spring options for her column. Even though they hadn't reached fall yet, the industry was always looking ahead at least one or two seasons. They had to stay ahead of other competing journalists, bloggers and magazines. The entire industry was one big race to see who could reveal the next season's hottest styles, fashions, dinner party themes and so much more.

"I'd like to document your journey to the aisle," Melissa stated with much more glee than Josie was feeling.

Josie stared down at the ruby. She couldn't stop staring at it. When she worked, there it was. When she drove, there it was. When she was sipping her morning coffee, there it was.

Always a reminder of this farce she'd started.

"I've got so much other material to cover," Josie stated. "I'm super excited about the fall spread I'm doing on various ciders and pairings. I think it will be great to incorporate those with a coastal feel since not everyone can have a bonfire and hoodies."

"Yes, yes," her editor agreed. "I love that idea, too, but I'd like to hand that one off and have you solely focus on this engagement."

Josie closed her eyes and took a deep breath. What could she say? Until the Manhattan opening, she and Reese were playing the part of lovers in love.

She had the lover part down, but she didn't know about the "in love" part.

Did she?

No. That would be silly. They weren't in love; they were just friends. Sure she loved him in that best-friend way, but what did she know about being in love with someone? She'd never experienced any such emotion.

She blew out her breath and attempted to relax. Once this was all over, she wouldn't be so anxious and have to take so many calming breaths…she hoped.

"That's fine," Josie reluctantly agreed.

She'd still get that fall piece back once Melissa realized there wasn't actually going to be a wedding, so there was nothing to worry about. Josie would just keep those notes saved on her computer and continue to work silently on that project.

"Would you be opposed to me sending a photographer with you when you look at dresses?" she asked. "Obviously, not taking shots when you find the one."

Dresses? Um, she wasn't going to go quite that far in this charade.

"I won't be looking at dresses for a while." Josie felt a little better about that true statement. "Reese is so busy with his opening in Manhattan, and we are taking a short trip to Tennessee before that. We can discuss the dress situation when I return."

And that would buy the time she needed to come clean.

"I can work with that time frame, but we'll need to post some things on the blog. Maybe you could share some of your favorite places where you'll be registering or we could do a fun poll on where viewers think you should honeymoon."

Registering and honeymoons were definitely not on her radar. Josie wanted out of this conversation and off the phone so she could start packing for her trip. She was both anxious and excited to go away with Reese. She wanted to meet Nick and Sam and she was more than ready to get away.

"Maybe a poll of favorite flowers?" Josie suggested. "Something simple, but not too much."

"Great idea. I'll get something put up tomorrow, but make sure you interact with the viewers." Her editor laughed. "Why did I tell you that? Of course you will. This is the happiest time of your life."

Josie glanced to the ring again. Maybe not the happiest, but definitely the most interesting.

"I'll be sure to hop on over the next few days," Josie promised.

She finally ended the call and sat back in her chair.

Pushing aside all the wedding talk and engagement whirlwind was going to be best for this trip. None of this was real, so letting it occupy space in her mind would only drive her crazy.

Josie came to her feet and shifted her focus to the trip. She needed to be Reese's support system for this. When he'd told his parents, Josie had been surprised at how well they took the news that Reese had discovered the truth. She'd been overcome with emotion at their precious bond, at the hurdles they faced as a team and conquered together.

She shouldn't feel sorry for herself. Maybe her

entire life would've been different had her mother lived, but that was not the way things were meant to be. Josie knew her father loved her. He just had closed in on himself and become even more regimented since he'd retired from the military, and that was okay. She could look back now and see that he had struggled. Everyone dealt with loss differently.

Josie headed to the bedroom she had been sharing with Reese. The work on her house was almost done, but she wouldn't be staying there until she and Reese returned from New York. When they returned, the farce would be over, the engagement would end and they'd go back to being just friends.

The looming deadline weighed heavy on her. She didn't know why. They'd been friends before; they'd be friends again.

But now that she'd been intimate with him, how could she give that up? They'd grown closer than she'd ever thought possible. But there was no future for them as an actual couple. There was no reason to be delusional about the truth.

Nope. Reese would go right back into that best-friend box and one day they would look back at this engagement and just laugh.

Right?

Thirteen

Reese slid his hand into Josie's as they made their way toward the entrance of Hawkins Distillery. This time walking in was no easier than the first, but at least now he had her by his side.

True, he'd already met the guys, but now there were more details to discuss and their lives would continue to intertwine.

Sam had arranged for a private dinner after closing hours so they would all have privacy and could freely talk. Apparently, Sam's and Nick's significant others were going to be here as well, so Reese was doubly glad he wouldn't be the fifth wheel.

"I've never heard you this quiet," she murmured as they neared the main entrance.

"How can you hear me being quiet?"

She laughed and slapped his arm. "You know what I mean."

He did and he appreciated her concern. Giving her hand a gentle squeeze, he stepped to the entrance and gripped the wrought iron door handle as he turned to face her.

"I know what you mean, but I'm fine. Nervous, but it helps that you're here." He tipped his head, his eyes darting to her lips. "You still haven't worn that red lipstick. Saving it for a special occasion?"

She rolled her eyes. "I can't just wear red lipstick, Reese."

"You can," he countered. "We all have to face our fears, Jo. Step out of our comfort zone sometimes to see what or who we can become."

Josie stared at him, then leaned in and gently kissed him before easing back. It took quite a bit to surprise Reese, but her spontaneous show of affection, when they didn't need to put on a show or weren't heading into the bedroom, surprised him.

"Since you're facing your fear, you looked like you needed it," she told him with a smile before he could question her.

Releasing the door, he framed her face and gave her a proper kiss. There was no gentleness, no lead-in. This woman was an addiction he couldn't let go of anytime soon.

When he eased back, still holding on to her,

her eyes remained closed and her mouth open. He stroked his thumb across her lower lip.

"I always need that," he murmured.

Her lids slowly lifted as she refocused on him. "What's happening between us?"

A knot in his stomach tightened. He had no clue how to answer that because he wasn't quite sure himself. He knew she was his best friend, knew that they were more than compatible in the bedroom and knew she'd always stood by his side. But he wasn't sure beyond that. In his world right now, he had a mess that needed to be cleaned up before he could think too much about anything else.

"Let's curb this topic for later," he suggested.

She stared another minute before ultimately nodding. He kissed her once more before letting her go and opening the door. He gestured for her to go ahead of him and then he followed her in.

"Wow," she muttered as soon as they were inside.

Reese had to admit, the place was spectacularly done in an industrial, modern yet old-charm combination. The exposed brick walls, scarred wood floors, and leather-and-metal chairs in the lobby area were perfect. Definitely masculine, rustic, very Smoky Mountains and spot-on for a distillery.

"I've never been to a distillery," she told him. "I may just have to do an article on Hawkins because this place is amazing, and I only just walked in. Think I could get a guided tour?"

"Of course you can."

Reese turned to see Sam striding toward them. He reached out and shook Reese's hand, then turned his attention to Josie.

"I'm Sam Hawkins," he stated. "I'll give you a tour anytime you want. After dinner, if you have the time."

Josie's smile widened and nodded. "I'm Josie and I'd love that, but I should tell you I'm a journalist, so I ask all the questions."

Sam laughed and folded his arms across his chest. "I'm aware of who you are, and you can ask all the questions you want."

Of course Sam had done his research. He'd invited virtual strangers into his space, strangers who were near family. Reese had done his share of looking into all parties in attendance as well.

Sam's fiancée, Maty Taylor, was an attorney. Actually, she had been Rusty's attorney, so Reese had to assume that's how Maty and Sam met.

Then there was Nick and his fiancée, Silvia Lane. Silvia was expecting a baby and the two were finishing up a spectacular resort in the mountains. Reese had every intention of booking their best suite once it opened.

"We'll discuss a possible article later," Josie promised.

Sam nodded. "Sounds good. Everyone is already in the back if you guys want to follow me."

Josie slid her hand into Reese's. The fact that he didn't even have to ask for her support just proved how in tune they were with each other. He might be a bundle of nerves on the inside, but having her with him during the most difficult, worrisome time in his life was absolutely invaluable.

They headed all the way into the back where a large enclosed dining area had been set up. The three exterior walls were all windows, providing a breathtaking view of the mountains.

"This is our main tasting room." Sam directed his comment to Josie. "I can set you up with a tasting after the tour, too, or you can try anything you want with your dinner."

Josie's smile beamed once again and Reese could feel the excitement rolling off of her. This was why she excelled at her job. She truly loved what she did, and it showed through her enthusiasm and her research.

Reese turned his attention to the other three in the room. They stood in a group near the table all set up and he found that their smiling faces put his nerves at ease. Instinct had gotten him far in business and he had a good feeling about today, about the future.

"You must be Reese and Josie." A slender woman with long blond hair approached them and extended her hand. "I'm Maty Taylor, Sam's fiancée. We're really glad you both could join us."

The other two came around the table as well, and

Reese felt the nerves slip away as all of the intro-
ductions were made. There was something so ironic
that the three men were all broad and powerful and
each of the women they were with appeared to be
bold, confident. Reese wondered what other underlying similarities they all shared.

"I'm Nick Campbell and this is my fiancée, Silvia Lane."

Silvia had a small baby bump and Reese felt a
twinge of jealousy. What would Josie look like pregnant with his child?

But immediately, he shut that question down.
He wasn't ready for long-term with her or anyone
else. He and Josie were forging their way through
this new territory and the thought of a child terrified him.

That one-day-family idea he'd had wasn't coming anytime soon. He had too many plans he wanted
to have in place before he started thinking about
his legacy.

"I have to be honest," Maty said, leaning toward
Josie. "Silvia and I are giddy with excitement that
you're here. We absolutely love your column."

Reese watched as Josie simply beamed. "Thank
you so much. I love meeting readers one-on-one.
Writing can be a lonely industry."

"And congratulations on the engagement," Silvia
added. "Isn't it funny how life works? The guys all

discover they're brothers and we all have recently become engaged."

Josie glanced to Reese and he literally saw the proverbial shield come down, masking her true emotions. Nobody knew her like he did, so her reaction wouldn't be noticeable. Still, he hated they were in a position to lie.

He also hated that he'd heard Chris had still been leaving notes and flowers on Josie's doorstep. His construction crew had kindly informed Reese of that fact, and Reese had sent Chris a not-so-subtle text telling the guy to move on or face harassment charges.

Hopefully that was the end of the issue.

The women seemed to shift and congregate discussing weddings and babies…neither topic appealed to Reese, so he moved toward Nick and Sam.

"Thanks for making the trip," Nick said. "I'm sure this is still a shock to you."

Reese tucked his thumbs through his belt loops and nodded. "I'm getting used to the idea. I spoke with my parents, so that was the toughest part."

"I can't imagine," Nick added. "Sam and I have a meeting set up with Rusty tomorrow evening at seven. We're actually meeting in his office."

Reese listened to the details about how the charges of embezzlement were sticking, how Rusty was about to lose everything and how Sam had never revealed to Rusty that he was Sam's father.

"So Rusty only knows of you?" Reese asked Nick. Nick nodded.

"I didn't want anything from him," Sam chimed in. "I didn't want money or to merge our businesses, nothing. I didn't want to give him any inkling that I was his son, but after thinking it over, I don't care if he knows. He's tried to buy my distillery for years now and I'm more than happy to show him just how powerful I've become. He's got nothing on me."

Well, Rusty was in for one hell of a surprise when he discovered he had two more bouncing baby boys.

Laughter from the women filtered through the open space and Reese couldn't help but smile. Josie fit into every single aspect of his life. He wondered what that kiss meant earlier, the one just outside when she'd claimed it was because he needed it.

Was she developing stronger feelings? Was he?

He glanced over his shoulder and she happened to glance his way. She sent him a wink that packed a punch, but not of lust. There was something building between them, something he wasn't sure he was ready for.

Regardless of what happened once their two-week sham was over, Reese knew he would never be the same.

"That was so much fun," Josie exclaimed as she and Reese made their way into the cabin they'd rented. "I cannot believe I got a tour, a tasting and an invite to come back to watch firsthand production."

Reese unlocked the door and ushered her inside the spacious mountainside cottage. Well, this particular cabin was called "Cozy Cottage" but there was nothing tiny about the four-thousand-square-foot space. Josie didn't realize how much she would love the mountains until she and Reese had driven up to this secluded rental. No wonder people always wanted to vacation here.

She might be a beach girl at heart, but she had a feeling the mountains would be calling her name again and again.

"And here I was worried you'd feel left out," Reese joked as he tossed his keys onto the table by the front door. "Sam seemed pretty anxious to let you interview him for a piece."

Josie smoothed her hair back and crossed her arms. "You're not jealous, are you?"

Reese held her gaze and cocked his head. "Should I be? Sam was named one of Tennessee's most eligible bachelors not that long ago."

Josie took a step closer. "Well, I think he's pretty in love with Maty and I'm—"

She stilled. No, she wasn't in love.

That was absurd. She was just getting caught up in all of this engagement fiasco.

"You're what?" Reese prompted.

Josie dropped her arms and squared her shoulders. "I'm not looking for a man," she told him.

Reese reached for her, his hands already working the zipper hidden on the side of her dress. "Is that so? Well, I wasn't looking for this, either, but here we are."

What did that mean? She wanted to ask, but his hands were moving on her, ridding her of all her clothes as he walked her backward.

"Have you checked out the deck?" he asked, a naughty gleam in his eye and a cocky smile to match.

"No. Should I?"

Her hands went to the buttons of his black dress shirt and she had him out of it before he could answer.

"There's a hot tub," he told her, firmly settling his hands at the dip in her waist. "There's also a flatbed swing. Both perfect for stargazing."

Josie smiled, raking her fingertip over the lines of his abs. "Is that what you're undressing me for? Stargazing?"

"You shouldn't get into the hot tub with your clothes on," he said.

Josie let him lead her outside, where she finished undressing him. The wide deck did provide a spacious hot tub and on the other end, a wide bed on a swing, perfect for lounging with your lover.

And that's the word she'd been looking for all this

time. Reese had moved from best friend to lover, but she wasn't sure where his head was with all of this. What would happen once they decided to publicly call off the engagement? Would they still sneak a rendezvous here or there? Would he still want this physical intimacy? Because she wasn't sure she could give this up now that she'd experienced Reese.

"You're letting your mind take you away again," he accused.

Before she could defend herself, he picked her up and hauled her over his shoulder like she was nothing more than a blanket. Mercy, his strength was sexy.

He climbed into the hot tub and gently set her down. The warm water instantly had chill bumps popping up. He reached over and tapped a button, instantly turning the jets on…as if she needed more stimulation to her already-aroused body.

When he turned back to her, he had that look again, the one that promised she was in for a good time.

"About that kiss earlier," he started as he reached for her. He sat down and pulled her onto his lap, giving her no choice but to straddle him. "Want to tell me why you're kissing me when nobody was looking?"

Yeah, about that. She'd told him he looked like he needed it, but in reality, she'd just wanted to. The pull toward him was growing stronger and stronger. She'd had to make up something quick because she didn't want to reveal her true feelings…basically because she wasn't even sure what her true feelings were.

"Maybe I like kissing you," she said, looping her arms around his neck. "Maybe I'm enjoying myself with you, despite all the chaos around us."

His hands eased up her thighs and around to cup her backside. "We do seem to draw the attention to us, don't we?"

She leaned into him, her breasts flattening against his chest. How could he keep carrying on a conversation? Her body was ready to go and he seemed to be taking his time.

Josie shifted a little more until she settled over him at the exact spot she ached to be. With her eyes locked onto his, she sank down, smiling when he moaned and closed his eyes.

Being in control where Reese was concerned wasn't an easy task. The man thrived on staying dominant at all times. But now his head dropped back against the edge of the hot tub and Josie braced her hands on his shoulders as she began to move.

Reese lifted his head and closed his mouth over her breast. She bit down on her lip to keep from crying out. Between his hands, his mouth and that rock-hard body moving beneath hers—oh, and those jets—Josie wasn't going to last.

When his lips traveled up to her neck, Josie dropped her head back and arched her body into his. He murmured her name over and over as she rocked against him.

All too soon, her body started climbing. As much as she wanted to make this moment last, she was fighting a losing battle.

Reese kept one hand on her backside and gripped her neck with the other, easing her down so he could claim her lips. She threaded her fingers through his hair and let every wave of emotion wash over her, through her.

His body tightened beneath hers as he joined her. Josie kept herself wrapped all around him, taking in the passionate kiss as her body came down from the high.

Reese's hold lessened as he nipped at her bottom lip, then rested his forehead against hers. The water continued to pulse around them, relaxing Josie even more. She didn't want to move, didn't want to face reality. She only wanted to stay in this moment that seemed so right because all too soon she would have to face the fact that she had to let Reese slip back into that friend box.

But for now, for tonight, she was in his arms.

Tomorrow he would meet his biological father and Josie wanted to give him as much comfort and peace as possible…and she prayed she could keep her heart from tumbling into love for her best friend.

Fourteen

"Are you ready for this?" Sam asked.

The three brothers stood outside the Lockwood Lightning Distillery. The sun was just starting to set behind the mountains, the tours had all ended, and the place was closed. Rusty was expecting them and Reese had a ball of nerves in his gut.

"Are you ready?" he countered to Sam. "Rusty isn't aware that you're his son, either."

Sam shrugged. "I honestly don't care if he ever finds out about me, but I'll stand with you guys as a united front."

Reese could understand and respect that. They were all at different places in their lives, but ultimately the deathbed confession of one woman had brought them all here. He also understood why Nick's mother had sent those letters. She hadn't wanted her son to have no family once she was gone.

"Let's get this over with," Nick stated. "I don't like spending any more time with this bastard than necessary."

Reese had dealt with some shady jerks in business before, but he hadn't imagined someone could be as terrible as Rusty was rumored to be. Clearly, he was getting ready to find out.

Sam reached up and pressed the intercom button next to the side door of the offices. Seconds later the door clicked and Nick reached for it.

He opened and gestured. "After you guys."

Reese stepped inside and the mixed scents of leather and alcohol hit him. The atmosphere was quite different from Sam's distillery. Here things seemed older, definitely a vibe from twenty years ago, where Sam's distillery seemed fresh and cutting-edge with the older themes complementing the decor.

"Gentlemen."

Reese turned toward the staircase and stared up at the landing, at Rusty Lockwood. He seemed older, heavier, in person than the photos Reese had seen online. Or maybe Rusty was just tired and run-down after being arrested and investigated regarding some serious charges.

Having your life and company on the brink of collapse would certainly wreak havoc.

Rusty's eyes scanned the guys, but ultimately landed on Reese.

"Recruiting new allies?" he asked. "I don't even know him, so I doubt he wants to see my demise."

Sam snorted. "You're about to know him. Are you coming down or standing there lording over us?"

"Are you staying long or will this meeting be short?" Rusty asked as he started to descend the steps.

Reese's first impression was that the man didn't like that he was being overrun. He didn't even bother with an introduction, as most people would when meeting someone new. He clearly didn't have any positive feelings toward Sam or Nick.

"Trust us, we don't want to be here any longer than necessary," Nick stated. "But there are some things we need to discuss."

Rusty came to the bottom of the steps and crossed his arms over his chest.

Reese couldn't stand it another second. "I'm Reese Conrad," he said, extending his hand.

Rusty stared for a second before giving a firm shake. "I've heard your name. You own those restaurants."

Those restaurants, like there was something wrong with being a restaurateur. Like people didn't have to book reservations at least a month in advance for a table, and even longer for the private lounge.

Rusty clearly had the mentality that he was above everyone else.

"I own eight restaurants and I'm opening my ninth in New York this coming weekend," Reese amended.

Rusty grunted and turned to Nick. "So what's this all about?"

"You recall my mother left me a letter about you being my biological father."

Rusty nodded. "And?"

"She sent letters to two of my brothers as well," Nick added.

Reese watched as Rusty processed that statement, then the man turned toward Sam, then Reese. His eyes showed absolutely no emotion. Nick might as well have told him the sky was blue for the lack of surprise on his face.

"So is this a family reunion?" Rusty asked. "And how do I know any of this is true?"

Sam took a step forward. "I don't give a damn if you believe us or not. We're just letting you know that you do have children. We want to clear the air and you can decide what to do from here. I don't believe any of us are looking for fatherly advice or holiday invites."

"I'm actually going to offer to buy Lockwood Lightning from you," Nick stated.

Reese jerked his attention to Nick, who only had his sights set on Rusty. From the way Sam reacted, he was just as surprised by Nick's offer.

"Buy me out?" Rusty scoffed. "When hell freezes over."

Nick shrugged and slid his hands into his pockets. "I knew that would be your first reaction, but that's why you're failing right now. You aren't thinking like a businessman. Instead, you're letting your emotions override common sense."

Rusty glanced at each of them. "Is that why you all came here? To gang up on me and get me to sell? You think I'm just passing down all I've built because I supposedly fathered you?"

"Bloodlines have nothing to do with this decision," Nick amended. "You don't need to answer me now, but I will own this distillery."

"What do you know about running a distillery?" Rusty mocked. "You renovate buildings and sell them off for others to run."

"He doesn't know about distilleries," Sam agreed. "But I do, and I'll be his partner."

"You think I'd sell to either of you?" Rusty asked. "After I tried to buy you out for years and you turned me down? I supposed your third crony is going to want in on this, too?"

Reese shrugged. "Always looking to expand. I'd go into business with them."

Rusty puffed up his chest as he pulled in a breath. The buttons on his shirt strained against the movement.

"If that's all you guys wanted, you wasted your time." Rusty started to turn back to the steps, but stopped himself. "I won't sell my distillery to any of you and I'm not really looking for children who will inherit my legacy. You can see yourselves out. The door will automatically lock, so don't come back."

And with that warm parting, Rusty went back up the steps to his lair or office or hellhole.

Nick and Sam both turned to Reese and he honestly didn't know what to say about the anticlimactic, not to mention fast, meeting they'd just had.

"Well, I guess that settles that," Reese said. "Clearly, he doesn't care about his sons, so I'm done here."

Nick glanced toward the empty steps and back to his brothers. "I meant what I said. I'm going to buy this place. It was something I'd thought about, but the minute I saw him, I knew. If you guys want to join me, we'd make a hell of a team."

Reese didn't make rash business decisions, but this was one thought that held merit. An already-established distillery run by three brothers who had all already made names for themselves in the hospitality and real estate industries was a no-brainer.

"We should discuss this elsewhere," Sam stated as he started toward the main door. "Let's head to my place where we can talk. I have a feeling this is going to take some strategic planning."

Reese followed, already pulling out his phone to text Josie and tell her what had happened and where he was heading. Odd that his first instinct had been to contact her and not his parents, but he would talk to them in person. He missed Josie when he wasn't with her and wanted to fill her in on everything going on in his life.

After last night, between the hot tub and then falling asleep holding her on the swinging bed under the stars, Reese couldn't help but wonder if maybe he was ready for more. Maybe the thought of commitment and long-term had always scared him in the past because the right person hadn't come into his life.

But she had.

She'd been there all along.

As things started to settle in his personal life, maybe long-term included Josie as well. Maybe she was settling right into the spot she was meant to be.

Reese had so much to think about regarding his brothers and Josie. There was a whole host of things he needed to weigh in his head before he made any life-changing decisions.

One thing was certain, though: the life he'd been living only a few weeks ago no longer existed. He was facing a new chapter and hell if all of this didn't scare him to death.

* * *

"I put an offer in on a house here."

Josie shifted and turned over in the swing bed, shocked by Reese's words. They swayed as she moved.

"In Green Valley?" she asked.

With one arm braced behind his head, he toyed with the ends of her hair with his other hand. His eyes held hers and she truly wished they could stay right here forever.

But that was a fantasy. They were friends, doing each other a favor, and they'd tumbled into bed in the process.

It was as simple and complex as that.

He grinned. "What do you think of this place?"

"You put an offer in on this cabin?"

Reese tucked her hair behind her ear, then rested his hand over hers, which was on his chest. "I love this outdoor setup overlooking the mountains. The interior would need to be updated to my tastes, but that's just cosmetic. I love the layout and the setting."

"Was it for sale?"

His brows drew in. "Did it need to be? I want a second home and for the right price, I bet the owners would be all too happy to find another cabin to buy and use as a rental."

That was Reese. Find something, make a plan, obtain it. He'd done the same with his Manhattan restaurant. He wanted to move on to a broader customer base and he'd done it without thinking twice.

"I don't know what's going to happen with Sam and Nick or even if this distillery of Rusty's is even going to be an option, but I want to be present when I'm needed and I'm growing to really love the mountains."

Yeah, she was, too. This was their third night here. They were flying to Manhattan in the morning, but they'd shared some special memories here… memories she'd have to keep locked away once all this was over.

"I invited the guys and their fiancées to the opening," Reese went on. "They said they'd be there."

Josie smiled. "You're really bonding with them. I'm glad. You all seem to really mesh well together."

"It's like we're old friends," Reese stated. "It's strange, really, but I'm comfortable around them."

"Have you talked to your parents about them?" she asked.

He nodded. "I called them earlier while you were in the shower. They're happy for me, that I'm forming a relationship with Nick and Sam. They apologized for how the meeting with Rusty went and I realized I had no expectations for that meeting, so it's not like I'm let down. I have the greatest parents of all time."

Josie couldn't argue there, but she didn't want to get swept up in thoughts about her late mom or her absent dad. She wanted to focus on the positive and the happiness that was stemming from all of this chaos.

Reese's finger slid over the ring on her hand. She cringed, feeling like a fraud every time she looked at it.

"Why did you marry Chris to begin with?" he asked.

The words hung between them and Josie didn't want to give him the truth. If she gave him the truth, that would just be another shove away from being "just friends."

Risking more terrified her. She'd rather have Reese back in that friend zone than to keep moving toward something that could crumble. She wasn't the best with relationships; she'd never had anything serious that lasted, so what did she truly know?

"Jo," he prompted.

She blinked her focus back to him. "It was a rash decision."

"Obviously, but what snapped inside that head of yours and made you rush to the courthouse? You had only dated him a few months."

Maybe she *should* be honest. Maybe that would be the best therapy and they could discuss what exactly was going on with all of these emotions. They'd talk and figure out why it was best that they just remain friends.

"You were engaged," she stated simply. "It made

me realize that we were entering new chapters in our lives."

She stared down at him, wondering how he'd take her response. But that was the truth. She'd realized she might not be the only woman in his life forever. There would be someone else he'd share secrets or inside jokes with.

And she had gotten jealous.

There. Fine. She could admit it…to herself. She was human and she didn't like sharing, okay?

"Making a rush in judgment isn't like you," he told her. "You plan everything. Hell, you have an alarm to check your planner. But you married some-one because I was engaged?"

"I made a mistake," she defended herself, sitting up a little more. She crossed her legs in front of her, needing just a bit of distance between them in this small space. "I wasn't in love with Chris. He was a nice guy, I feel terrible that I hurt him, but honestly I don't think he loved me, either. He just wanted to be married because his family had been putting pressure on him."

Completely the truth.

"Why did you get engaged?" she retorted.

Reese shrugged and stared up at the starry sky. "I was taking over Conrad's full time and starting to wonder about my legacy and who I would share it with. I know I want a family someday, but once I got engaged, I realized I wasn't ready and she wasn't the one."

Josie placed her hand on his chest and smiled. "Sounds like we both dodged bigger mistakes."

"Speaking of, Chris has been leaving notes and stopping by your house," he told her. "My contractor informed me several days ago, so I reached out to Chris."

Josie stilled. "What? You should let me take care of this."

Reese's gaze came back to hers. "I let you try that, we ended up engaged and he still didn't back off. I told him if there was any further contact there would be harassment charges filed."

Josie didn't want a keeper. She didn't want anyone, especially Reese, fighting her battles.

"This engagement wasn't my doing," she informed him. "I told Chris I had moved on. You're the one who threw out I was your fiancée."

"He needed something stronger than just dating," Reese replied in that calm tone of his. "I could've said we'd already eloped."

Josie pulled in a deep breath and closed her eyes. The opening was in just a couple days and then they would go back to normal. Hopefully Chris would still keep his distance.

"I'm tired," she told Reese as she rolled off the side of the swing and came to her feet. "I'm going in to bed."

Reese continued to lie there, staring up at her. "We can stay out here," he suggested. "When I buy this place, I plan on staying out here as much as possible."

Josie smiled, but her heart was heavy.

She wanted things to go back to the way they were a few weeks ago. She wanted to ignore the way her heart shifted when Reese talked about lying with her, holding her or when he spoke of the future. They didn't have a future, not in the way they'd been playing house these past several days.

"You can stay out here," she told him. "I'll be fine."

She turned and stepped into the house, closing the patio door behind her. Maybe he'd come in and maybe he wouldn't. Right now, she needed time to think.

Reese had never acted like he wanted more with her. He seemed content with just the physical, which was fine. It had to be. If they tried this whole relationship for real, she didn't know how long that could or would last. If he tired of her and moved on...that would definitely ruin their friendship.

That was a risk she couldn't take, no matter how much she might be falling for her best friend.

Fifteen

Reese adjusted his tie, more out of nerves than anything else. The opening was due to kick off in less than thirty minutes, but that wasn't what had a ball of tension in his belly.

The restaurant business was in his blood; he wasn't worried in the slightest about failure or mishaps. Manhattan had been his main goal and here he was. Getting the building in the exact location he wanted had been the most difficult part. Everything from here on out was in his wheelhouse.

He stood on the second-floor balcony where he had a clear view of the first-floor entrance and one of the bars. For this location, he'd gone with old-world charm. Black and white, clean lines, clear bulbs suspended from the second floor to the first, a glossy mahogany bar. He'd wanted to keep this place upscale like the others, but really appeal to that classical era he associated with New York.

Josie had accompanied him from the penthouse he'd purchased a month ago. He wanted to keep a place in town because he planned on visiting quite often now. Their conversations had been a little strained since they'd left Green Valley a couple days ago. She was pulling back, and he was losing her.

The fear that continued to grow and develop inside him stemmed from that distance, from this fake engagement, from the fact that after tonight they wouldn't have to pretend anymore.

He'd just wanted to get through this opening, but now…well, he wasn't so sure he wanted things to end.

Oh, she wanted to go back to the friendship they'd once had, but that was impossible now. He knew her too intimately, had let her into that pocket of his heart he hadn't even known existed, and he'd seen her in a whole new light.

After being best friends for twenty years, Reese hadn't even known it was possible to still learn more about her, but he had. He'd actually discovered more about himself, too.

Like the fact that he wanted to give this relationship a go in every way that was real.

A flash of red caught his eye and he turned his attention to the bar area below. He knew that inky black hair and those killer curves.

But red?

When they'd arrived, she'd been wearing a long black gown with a high neck and an open back. This dress was…damn. This was the hottest thing he'd ever seen. That dip in the back scooped dangerously low, and when she turned, he got an eyeful of a deep vee in the front as well. Classy, sexy and a hell of a shock to his entire system.

Hadn't he just thought that he'd finally seen all sides of Josie?

She glanced around the open space and he couldn't maintain the distance another minute. He made his way down the steps from the VIP area and crossed the tile floor.

"This is not the same woman who came with me," he stated.

Josie spun around, a wide smile on her face. Her dress wasn't the only thing red—she had her lips painted and it was all Reese could do to contain himself and not cover her mouth and mess that all up.

Damn, she was the sexiest thing he'd ever seen—and for the time being, fake or otherwise, she was his.

"I wanted to surprise you, so I had some things sent over so I could change here," she told him. "And

I figured if I was going to go all out, I might as well do it all."

She gave a slow spin with her arms out wide. "What do you think? Can I pull off color?"

He took a step closer and reached for her hips. "I think I'm going to have to cut this night short and get you alone as soon as possible."

That red smile widened. "You can't mess me up, so keep those lips and hands to yourself. I have a dutiful hostess role to play as my fiancé is having a grand opening."

"He's a lucky bastard," Reese murmured as he leaned in and grazed his lips up the side of her neck.

She shivered beneath his touch and his grip on her hips tightened.

"We still have time," he whispered into her ear.

The waitstaff bustled around getting last-minute flutes of champagne and appetizers set out at various tables, but if they saw him and Josie in a passionate embrace, that would just make them look like more of a couple.

And right now, he didn't care who saw him doing what. He wanted her alone and he wanted her now.

"Other than the fact I want to rip that dress off and show you how much I need you, you do look so damn amazing, Jo."

She looped her arms around his neck. "I feel… good. I was worried once I got here I'd chicken out and keep on the black dress, but once I slid into this, it felt right."

He took a step back before he made a complete fool of himself and took her hands in his. His thumb slid over her ring.

"And it matches perfectly," he told her.

Her smile faltered a bit.

"What is it?" he asked.

Her eyes went from their joined hands back up to his face. "Have you seen the blog?" she asked. "It's up now. I just scanned through it when I was in the back."

"I haven't seen it," he told her. "Is something wrong with it?"

She pursed her lips for a moment before shaking her head. "No, nothing wrong. It just looks so real. Even I almost believe we're engaged."

Reese's breath caught, but he quickly recovered. Taking her hand, he ushered her off to the side where nobody could overhear. He kept his hands firmly locked with hers because he wanted to get this out; he wanted her to listen to everything he had to say.

Mercy, this was the riskiest move he'd ever made and he didn't care. If he let this moment, this woman, go without speaking his mind, then he'd regret it forever.

"You're scaring me with that look in your eye," she joked.

"What would you say to keeping the ring?" he asked.

Her brows drew in. "You insisted I keep it when I told you to return it. You claimed it could be my birthday gift, but it's a bit extravagant for that."

Reese swallowed the lump in his throat. "It's not extravagant if it's a real engagement ring," he suggested. "Keep it, keep me. Let's do this, Jo."

Her eyes widened on her gasp and she jerked her hands from his. "Do this? You mean, stay engaged?"

His delivery and proposal really needed work, but he was so damn nervous he hadn't really prepared his exact words.

"When we were talking the other night, it occurred to me that maybe we hadn't found the right people because we *are* the right people."

Josie continued to stare at him like he'd lost his mind, and maybe he had, but he still had to take this chance.

"Think about it," he went on. "We have always been there for each other. No matter what has happened, good or bad, we have each other's backs. Right? We trust each other. We're a hell of a team in bed and out."

"But you're my best friend," she countered, her voice holding no conviction. "We agreed…"

He took a step closer. "That was before everything changed. I love you, Josie."

"I love you, too," she said. "*As my best friend.* We

can't do this, Reese. Just because we grew intimate doesn't mean we can build a life together."

"Your fear is showing," he murmured. "We've already built a life together."

"My fear?" she questioned. "It's common sense. We wouldn't know how to live together, to really forge our lives together like a husband and wife. Have you really thought about this or did you just get caught up in the role?"

"The only thing I've gotten caught up in is you. You can't believe I would ask if I wasn't serious. I want to try this with you."

Her eyes misted as she took another step back. "Trying leaves room for failure, and I love you too much to lose you as my friend, Reese. I'm sorry."

She turned and walked toward the back of the restaurant, leaving him completely confused and shattered.

He'd known before he'd asked that she'd be scared, but he'd had no clue she would completely shut him down. Did she really believe he'd let her get hurt? Didn't she trust him, trust *them*, more than that?

Chatter from the front doors pulled his attention back to the moment. Nick, Silvia, Sam and Maty were all smiles as they were the first to arrive. Right behind them, his parents.

This was his family. All of these people right

here were here to support him on the most important night of his life.

Josie might have had to put distance between them, and that was fine, but he would regroup and stick around.

He wasn't going anywhere now that he knew exactly what he wanted...*who* he wanted.

Josie smiled and nodded, she shook hands and answered questions. Nobody knew the truth, that her insides were shaking, that her head was ready to explode with all the thoughts ramming together in there, and her heart was aching in a way she'd never known.

How dare Reese spring that on her? A real engagement? Was he out of his ever-loving mind?

"You look absolutely stunning."

Josie turned to see Silvia and Maty. The two women were beaming, which lightened Josie's mood somewhat. She needed a distraction and perhaps these were just the ladies she needed to chat with.

"I know you always wear black for your column and appearances," Maty stated, "but that red is gorgeous with your dark hair and skin tone."

"Thank you," Josie said, sipping her champagne. "I was worried it was too over-the-top, but I wanted to do something special for Reese. He's always on me about stepping out of my comfort zone."

Is that why he'd proposed for real? To get her

out of that comfort zone? Because that wasn't just stepping out, that was jumping off a cliff without a parachute.

"I just saw the blog right before we came in." Silvia clutched her glass of sparkling water and leaned in to Josie. "Girl, you two are so adorably in love. I can't wait to see your journey to the aisle."

"I still can't believe we're all getting married," Maty said with a wide grin. "It's such an exciting time."

Josie wanted to correct them; she wanted to confide in someone that this was all a farce and there was no way she could marry Reese.

He didn't actually mean what he'd said. He'd gotten caught up, that's all. He would realize once he had time to come down from this high of the opening that they were better off as friends.

That nice, safe zone they'd lived in for so long was just waiting for them to return. Josie wanted that normalcy back because being in limbo with her emotions, her hormones, her heart…it was simply too much to bear.

She'd felt so brave wearing this red gown, but when it came to her feelings regarding Reese, she wasn't feeling so bold anymore. She'd tried. She wanted to be that daring woman. But…what if the risk was too great? What if they destroyed the life they'd built during all those years of friendship?

"I see the guys are talking with Reese's mom and

dad." Josie nodded to the bar area. "I'm so glad this is all working out for him."

Silvia nodded. "Nick was worried if the third brother came forward that he would be like Rusty. I'm just grateful they've all found one another. Nick said he's going to do everything in his power to buy out Rusty, and Sam and Reese are joining forces."

Reese had mentioned that to Josie. She couldn't believe he was adding more business ventures to his plate, but that was Reese. He lived for success and to her knowledge, he'd never failed at anything.

Maybe that's why he didn't want to let her go. Would he see this public announcement calling off their engagement as a failure, like she had said at the start?

"Is everything all right?" Maty asked, placing a hand on Josie's arm.

Josie blinked back to the moment. "Oh, yes. Sorry about that. It's been a long couple of weeks."

Understatement.

"Would you two excuse me?" she asked.

The ladies nodded and Josie stepped aside to go get some fresh air or a moment to herself. Even with all the chaos of the successful opening, she was having a difficult time concentrating on anything other than this ring weighing so heavy on her hand.

The ring that Reese wanted to mean more than it could.

Josie made her way to the private office Reese

kept in the back. Once inside, she closed the door and leaned back against it. She just needed a minute to compose herself, that's all. Then she could go back and play the dutiful, proud fiancée.

Because at midnight, this Cinderella story was over.

Sixteen

Reese stood on the second-floor balcony once again, staring down onto the empty first floor. The launch had been a huge success. The reservations were all booked up for the next three months and several reviewers were already talking about them during some prime spots on their social media accounts.

He wondered if Josie took mental notes or if she'd just checked out after he'd dropped that bomb on her.

Reese trusted her. He knew she'd still cover the event and make a good article for *Cocktails & Classy*.

Which reminded him, he still hadn't seen their

post on the blog. Part of him didn't want to see it, if the images had impacted Josie so much. Was that why she'd been so scared? She'd seen the photos and realized what they had was real?

Reese pulled his cell from his pocket and quickly found the site. He skipped the dialogue; he knew exactly what they'd said during their interview. That had been the easy part.

The first image he came to was the one where Josie had her eyes closed, her head turned toward her shoulder and he had placed a kiss on her head. The tender, delicate picture made him smile.

He scrolled through more words and stopped when he came across the picture of when they had to lean in for the "almost" kiss. His fingertips splayed over her jawbone and neck as he tipped her head back. Josie's eyes were locked onto his, her lips slightly parted.

Even though he'd been right there in that moment, he'd had no clue what this shot had actually looked like. They definitely looked like they were in love, like they were literally half a breath away from closing that narrow gap between them. She'd been nervous, worried what this would do to them.

If only she'd let those fears go and see what she had right in front of her.

Heels clicked on the tile below and Reese glanced from his phone to see Josie step into view. She immediately glanced up and caught his gaze.

"I thought you took a ride back to the penthouse," he told her.

"I was going to, but I couldn't leave."

Reese glanced from the phone back to her. "I was just looking at the announcement online. We look good."

She crossed her arms over her chest, giving him a delicious view from this angle.

"We do," she agreed.

The tension in that vast gap between them was charged and Reese felt it best to keep a good distance. If he got too close, he'd want to touch her, hold her, tell her every reason why they should be together, but she had to come to that realization on her own.

"I know you think it's a good idea to keep going," she started. "But I can't marry you, Reese."

So they were still at that stalemate. Fine. He was a patient man and Josie was worth waiting for.

"You have to understand," she added.

"I understand you're afraid. I understand this isn't what you had planned, but you have to see that none of this is new."

She jerked like he'd surprised her. "Not new? We've only been faking this for two weeks and we've crammed quite a bit into that short time frame. It's all quite new."

He couldn't stand the distance anymore. Reese came down the steps and stood at the bottom of the landing, his eyes meeting hers across the way. She still wore that red dress, those red lips. She still took his breath away whether she had on black, red or nothing at all.

"None of this is new," he explained. "Everything between us has always been there. We are just now bringing it to the surface."

Her arms dropped to her sides as she shook her head. Her fear and hesitancy made him want to reach for her, but he also recognized he needed to give her some space.

She glanced down to her hand as she toyed with the ring. He stared, knowing what was coming, hoping he was wrong.

But she slid the ring off and held it out in her palm. When her eyes came up to meet his, there was no way she could hide the unshed tears.

"I'm not taking it back," he told her. "I bought it for you."

"You never bought me something this expensive for my birthday before."

He stared at her for another minute, but knew which battle he wanted to fight. He didn't want to be a jerk about this, and she obviously needed time to think. Fine. He'd hold it for her until she was ready.

Sliding the ring into his pocket, he extended his hand.

"How about we head up to the rooftop, take a bottle of champagne and relax?" he suggested. "We've both had a rough few weeks and I could use some quiet."

She looked at his hand, then back to his face; her brows drew in as she cocked her head.

"That's it?" she asked. "We're just going to move past the fact that you wanted to marry me and now we're going back to being buddies that fast?"

Damn woman was confusing him…and herself, which was probably a good thing. If she was confused, then that meant her mind wasn't completely made up.

"Isn't that what you wanted?" he asked. "I still need my best friend. Do I want more? Of course. But I'm not pushing you out of my life simply because we don't agree on the future."

Her lips curved into a grin as she reached for his hand. "One glass," she told him. "And no sex."

She was killing him.

"That dress was made for sex," he informed her, leading her to the elevator.

As they stepped into the elevator, she slid her hand from his. "I can't, Reese. As much as I want you physically, I can't risk my heart. I need a clean break from this, or someone is going to end up hurt."

Too late. Her rejection stung, but he wasn't giving up and he had to believe she wanted more and was just too worried to grab hold of what was right in front of her.

Her actions said more than her words ever could.

She'd stepped out of her structured life to take a chance with him; she'd worn the red dress, the red lipstick…she did want to be bold and brave, but he knew she was afraid.

He respected her and knew she would realize what they had… eventually.

"Fine," he conceded. "Champagne on the rooftop with our clothes on to celebrate a successful night."

She nodded. "Deal."

Reese led her up to the rooftop with flutes and an unopened bottle. If she wanted to slide back into friend territory, then that's what they'd do. He hoped she realized he never backed down from a fight, and having Josie permanently in his life was the one fight he would never give up.

Josie stared at the blue bikini. Should she? She was home in her own element and going to her own private beach. Who would even care? Besides, she'd donned that red dress for everyone to see and she had to admit, she'd felt pretty damn good about it.

After flying back to Sandpiper Cove, Josie had moved back into her own home since the renovations were done. The crew had put everything back the way it had been before. Her spare closet needed to be reorganized, but at least the mess was completely gone and nothing had been ruined.

Josie needed to spend the day on the beach, to decompress after a whirlwind trip, meeting Reese's new family in Tennessee, his opening in New York and the proposal that never should've happened.

It shouldn't have…right?

Yes. She had made the right decision to save them further hurt down the road. Not only the hurt, but she was also saving them from destroying a friendship that she could never replace. He was her one constant. She needed him to always be there, and if they married and decided it didn't work or he grew tired of her, where would she be?

Alone with only her work to keep her company.

Josie stripped from her pajamas and pulled on the blue bikini. To hell with it. For two weeks she'd been so happy. Perhaps that was due to taking chances and being that bold woman she'd always thought she could be, a bold woman like her mother had been.

She grabbed the matching sheer cover and her straw hat. After sliding into a pair of gold sandals, she stepped from the closet and caught herself in the mirror. Well, she didn't look terrible, just different. But she was keeping it and spending the day in the sun, with a cold beverage and a good book.

Though with the way her mind was spinning, she wasn't sure any book could hold her attention.

The alarm from her driveway dinged. Who would be coming here? She wasn't expecting anybody.

Reese. Had to be.

She glanced at her reflection one more time, but decided not to change. He'd seen her in a bikini countless times over the years. Just because they'd been intimate didn't mean she had to do things differently. They were back to being just friends and a bikini was something she'd wear with a friend. Besides, this was her house. She could wear whatever she wanted without worrying about unexpected guests.

Josie headed down the hall and to the foyer just in time to see Chris pull his car up near the steps. On a sigh, she pulled her wrap around her and stepped onto the porch.

The second he got out of his car, he caught sight of her. Thankfully, he remained in the drive and didn't make his way to her.

"I'm not going to bother you," he promised with his hands up. "I just wanted to come by and tell you I'm happy for you."

Confused, Josie took another step until she was at the edge of the porch. "You couldn't text?"

"After all we've been through, I needed to see you one last time. I saw the blog and I realized that you and Reese have something I could never have with you. As much as I hate it and wish we were still together, I know you two belong together. Too bad we didn't realize that sooner."

She didn't know what to say, so she remained silent.

"Anyway, congratulations," he stated. "You deserve to be happy."

Josie could tell he truly meant it. "Thank you. I want you to be happy, too, Chris."

He offered her a smile and stared another moment before he waved and got back into his car. She watched as he drove off and she wondered what he'd seen in those images that she hadn't. True, she'd stared at the blog longer than necessary; she'd even pulled it up again this morning.

She and Reese did look happy, but they *were* happy. They had a bond that was unmistakable. But they were going to have to discuss a mutual press release regarding their "breakup" and make it sound like they were still ridiculously happy and loved each other…they were just not in love.

The thought tugged at her heart and she pushed the emotion aside as she went back into her house. She reset the alarm and went to the kitchen to whip up a mai tai.

Just as she was pouring her blended drink into a large travel cup, her cell rang. Josie sat everything down and reached across the island to her phone.

Not Reese. How silly that she'd been expecting him to call or come by. True, they'd just gotten in yesterday, but it'd been over twelve hours since she'd seen him.

Her editor's name lit up the screen and Josie knew she still had to pretend the engagement was on.

"Hello."

"Jo, the blog is breaking records," Melissa squealed.

"Have you seen? The comments are astounding and we are getting emails that we can't keep up with."

When she'd gotten online this morning, she hadn't even looked at the comments—she'd been too wrapped up in the photos.

"That's great news," Josie stated.

"We'd love to keep this momentum going," her editor tacked on. "Do you know when formal engagement pictures will be ready or when you will be dress shopping? If we could do a weekly wedding update, I think that would be best. There are so many details that we could easily make this work."

Josie rubbed her forehead. "Let me think about this, okay? Reese and I just got back last night and I'm still a bit fuzzy."

"Yes, of course. Oh, and honey, that red dress was fabulous," she praised. "Great move on your part to branch out at your fiancé's grand opening. You two looked absolutely perfect."

Guilt weighed heavy on her, but another emotion overrode the guilt. Regret.

Had she made the right decision turning Reese down? Since the moment she'd slid that ring off, everything had felt wrong, out of place.

"Thanks," Josie replied. "Let me think on weekly blogs and I'll be in touch."

"Sounds great. I'm just so happy for you guys. You really look like you're in love and that's so rare to find these days."

Unable to handle anymore, Josie said her good-byes and hung up. She grabbed her drink, ignored her phone on the counter and slid her beach bag from the kitchen chair and onto her shoulder.

No phone, no uninvited guests at her door; she just needed peace and quiet and the ocean. That's all. The space in her head was filled to capacity.

And the man who occupied each and every thought was the man who claimed to love her, who wanted to spend his life with her.

Josie pulled in a deep breath and headed out to the beach. She had so much thinking to do and serious decisions to make. Was she ready to take that leap? Was she ready to take the biggest risk of her life and create a brand-new box?

One where she and Reese were together forever?

Seventeen

A shadow came over her and Josie squealed.

"Good grief, Reese," she scolded as she jerked her legs over the side of her lounge chair. "You scared the hell out of me."

"Well, you scared me, because I've been texting and calling. Usually, you are glued to your phone."

She adjusted her hat and stared up at him. "I wanted some time alone and didn't want to be interrupted. What are you doing here?"

"I was going to see if you wanted to take the boat out?" he said. "Nick, Sam, Silvia and Maty are at my house."

"They are?" she exclaimed. "Did you know they were coming?"

"We had discussed it, but it was kind of a last-minute thing. I invited them yesterday before we left New York and they came this morning. Frisco is going to work up a shrimp and crab boil. I know how much you love that."

Josie came to her feet and reached for her cover-up, but too late. Reese's eyes raked over her barely clad body and every one of her nerve endings sizzled with arousal.

Well, clearly this was going to be a problem. Now that she'd had him, she couldn't simply turn off that need.

She slid her arms into the sheer material and stared back at him. "We aren't engaged anymore," she reminded him. "So how is this going to work?"

Reese shrugged. "I would have asked you as a friend even before we did this fake engagement. Nothing has changed there, Josie. I want my best friend by my side and I figured you'd enjoy the day out. You seemed to really hit it off with Maty and Silvia."

"I did. They're amazing."

Reese smiled and her heart ached. "So you'll come? I can take you over if you're ready now. It looks like you're all set for a day on the boat."

This was weird. He made no move to touch her. Except for that wandering gaze, she would swear he was right back in that friend zone.

Had he moved there so easily? Had he already forgotten that he'd told her he loved her?

Reese picked up her sunglasses and book and shoved them into her beach bag, then lifted it up.

"What do you say?" he asked.

What did she say? Josie shook her head, as if that would somehow put all these jumbled thoughts back into place.

Melissa thought she and Reese looked in love; her ex-husband had said the same. Reese professed his love and Josie…was confused.

"Something wrong?" he asked. "If you don't want to come, no pressure. We can tell them about this whole friend thing. Believe me, they're discreet with secrets, so they won't say anything until we can make an official statement."

Josie continued to stare at him. "That's it? Less than forty-eight hours ago you said you loved me and now you're good with being friends?"

"I do love you," he informed her without hesitation. "I also respect your decision. What do you want from me?"

The question was, what did she want from herself? She wanted to be able to trust her feelings, to trust that if she took this leap, he'd be holding her hand the entire way. She'd been slowly moving toward this moment, and now she was going to reach for the life she wanted…the life they deserved together.

"I want it all," she murmured before she could stop herself.

Her eyes dropped to her feet as a wave of fear coupled with relief washed over her.

She'd let out her true feelings, but now what?

Reese's fingertip slid beneath her chin as he forced her to meet his gaze. "Say that again, Jo. I didn't quite catch it."

She closed her eyes.

"No," he demanded. "Look at me. I've waited for this for a long time."

"How long?"

His smile softened. "Probably since I met you, but at least a few years."

Years? How had she taken so long to catch up?

"Tell me what you're thinking," he told her. "I don't want any confusion."

He still hadn't reached for her, so she reached for him. She placed her hands on either side of his face and stepped into him.

"As much as I love our friendship, I love you more," she told him. "All of you. I want to be with you, but I'm terrified."

"You think I'm not?" he asked with a laugh. "I just know that never having you again sounds like pure torture and I need you, Jo. I need you in my house, in my life, as more than a friend."

"What happens if we can't—"

He covered her lips with his. Her bag slipped to

the ground, landing at her feet as he wrapped his arms around her and pulled her flush with his body.

"We don't fail," he murmured against her lips. "That's not who we are, and we love each other too much."

Her fear melted away little by little. He was right. They were both so strong, they'd always held each other up and she knew going into a deeper relationship would be no different.

"So do we get the ring back on this finger?" he asked.

Josie nodded. "Yes. Let's go back to your house since your family is waiting on you."

"Our family," he corrected. "They're our family now, Jo, because you're mine."

Epilogue

Six months seemed like a long time, but in the grand scheme of things regarding legal doings and commercial sales, it was lightning fast.

Reese smiled. Lockwood Lightning was now officially under new ownership. Sam, Nick and Reese were in the moonshine business.

"This has been a hell of a ride," Nick stated as he poured five glasses of moonshine and one glass of apple cider for his very pregnant fiancée.

The guys had signed papers yesterday and this morning they were making things official. Rusty had been so strapped for cash between the embezzlement, the lawyer fees and back taxes he'd "forgotten" that he'd had no choice but to sell. The guys offered more than anyone else would have and now they were all starting this new chapter as one unit.

"I'm glad I could be part of it," Reese said, sliding his arm around Josie's waist.

Since that day she'd come home with him six months ago, she hadn't left. She'd sent for her things, moved in and they were officially planning a wedding. The weekly blogs were getting to be exhausting, but she was loving every minute of it and he wanted nothing more than to see her happy.

Nick doled out all of the glasses as they stood in a circle in the main tasting area of Lockwood Lightning.

"To new beginnings," Sam declared as he raised his tumbler. "This is just the start of a new dynasty."

"And with the resort opening in a few weeks, we are slowly taking over Tennessee," Nick added.

"I'll drink to that," Sam laughed.

Silvia gasped. "Oh, no."

Everyone turned to see her holding her side.

"I think I'm having a contraction." She grimaced. "I mean, I think I've had them all morning, but this one seems strong."

"All morning?" Nick asked. "And you're just now telling me?"

She scrunched her face and handed over her glass. Josie quickly reached for it before it dropped.

"I knew this was such an important moment for

you guys," she defended. "But I'm pretty sure I need to get to the hospital."

Reese nodded. "Go. We'll take care of things here."

Nick ushered Silvia out the door and Reese turned, catching Josie's eye. She smiled and something he didn't quite recognize glinted in her eye.

She tipped back the cider that had been Silvia's and handed him her moonshine.

"You might want to do another toast to new beginnings," she told him. "And I'll take another cider."

Her statement, her actions, finally hit him.

"Jo?"

Her smile widened and she nodded. "About ten weeks now."

"Ten weeks?"

"Surprise," she exclaimed.

Maty laughed and turned to Sam. "Don't look at me. I have no news, but I wouldn't mind getting a puppy."

"Deal," Sam agreed.

Reese took the empty glass from Josie and handed it to Sam. He pulled her against him and couldn't help the tears that clogged his throat. All these years he'd thought about a family, but never knew where to start.

Now he knew.

The woman he'd been waiting for had been in his life for so long. She'd agreed to marry him for real six months ago and now they were going to start a family. Nothing could have made him happier.

"I love you," he whispered into her ear.

"I love you, baby." She held on to him and he thought he heard a little sniff. "We're going to kill this parenting gig."

He eased back. "We are," he agreed. "But can we not tell your editor? I'm afraid of what she'll have us do next for the magazine."

Josie eased back, her eyes filled with unshed tears as she smiled. "We'll hold her off as long as possible."

Good, because Reese needed his family all to himself for now. He'd waited a long time and he finally had everything he'd ever wanted.

* * * * *

Meet all of the Lockwood Lightning brothers!

An Unexpected Scandal
Scandalous Reunion
Scandalous Engagement

WE HOPE YOU ENJOYED
THIS BOOK FROM

✛ HARLEQUIN
DESIRE

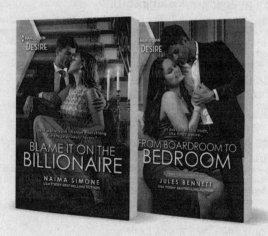

*Luxury, scandal, desire—welcome to
the lives of the American elite.*

Be transported to the worlds of oil barons, family dynasties,
moguls and celebrities. Get ready for juicy plot twists,
delicious sensuality and intriguing scandal.

6 NEW BOOKS AVAILABLE EVERY MONTH!

HDHALO2020

COMING NEXT MONTH FROM

HARLEQUIN

DESIRE

Available July 7, 2020

#2743 BLACK SHEEP HEIR
Texas Cattleman's Club: Rags to Riches • by Yvonne Lindsay
Blaming the Wingate patriarch for her mother's unhappiness, Chloe Fitzgerald wants justice for her family and will go through the son who left the fold—businessman Miles Wingate. But Miles is not what she expected, and the white-hot attraction between them may derail everything...

#2744 INSATIABLE HUNGER
Dynasties: Seven Sins • by Yahrah St. John
Successful analyst Ryan Hathaway is hungry for the opportunity to be the next CEO of Black Crescent. But nothing rivals his unbridled appetite for his closest friend, Jessie Acosta, when he believes she's fallen for the wrong man...

#2745 A REUNION OF RIVALS
The Bourbon Brothers • by Reese Ryan
After ending a sizzling summer tryst years ago, marketing VP Max Abbott doesn't anticipate reuniting with Quinn Bazemore—until they're forced together on an important project. He's the last person she wants to see, but the stakes are too high and so is their chemistry...

#2746 ONE LAST KISS
Kiss and Tell • by Jessica Lemmon
Working with an ex isn't easy, but successful execs Jayson Cooper and Gia Knox make it work. That is until they find themselves at a wedding where one kiss leads to one hot night. But will secrets from their past end their second chance?

#2747 WILD NASHVILLE WAYS
Daughters of Country • by Sheri WhiteFeather
Country superstar Dash Smith and struggling singer Tracy Burton were engaged—until a devastating event tore them apart. Now all he wants to do is help revive her career, but the chemistry still between them is too hard to ignore...

#2748 SECRETS OF A PLAYBOY
The Men of Stone River • by Janice Maynard
To flush out the spy in his family business, Zachary Stone hires a top cyber expert. When Frances Wickersham shows up, he's shocked the quiet girl he once knew is now a beautiful and confident woman. Will she be the one to finally change his playboy ways?

YOU CAN FIND MORE INFORMATION ON UPCOMING HARLEQUIN TITLES, FREE EXCERPTS AND MORE AT HARLEQUIN.COM.

HDCNM0620

SPECIAL EXCERPT FROM

(H) HARLEQUIN
DESIRE

*After ending a sizzling summer tryst years ago,
marketing VP Max Abbott doesn't anticipate reuniting
with Quinn Bazemore—until they're forced together on
an important project. He's the last person she wants
to see, but the stakes are too high and so is
their chemistry…*

Read on for a sneak peek at
A Reunion of Rivals *by Reese Ryan.*

"Everyone is here," Max said. "Who are we—"

"I apologize for the delay. I got turned around on my way back from the car."

Max snapped his attention in the direction of the familiar voice. He hadn't heard it in more than a decade, but he would never, *ever* forget it. His mouth went dry, and his heart thudded so loudly inside his chest he was sure his sister could hear it.

"Peaches?" He scanned the brown eyes that stared back at him through narrowed slits.

"Quinn." She was gorgeous, despite the slight flare of her nostrils and the stiff smile that barely got a rise out of her dimples. "Hello, Max."

The "good to see you" was notably absent. But what should he expect? It was his fault they hadn't parted on the best of terms.

Quinn settled into the empty seat beside her grandfather. She handed the old man a worn leather portfolio, then squeezed his arm. The genuine smile that lit her brown eyes and activated those killer dimples was firmly in place again.

He'd been the cause of that magnificent smile nearly every day that summer between his junior and senior years of college when he'd interned at Bazemore Orchards.

"Now that everyone is here, we can discuss the matter at hand."

His father nodded toward his admin, Lianna, and she handed out bound presentations containing much of the info he and Molly had reviewed that morning.

"As you can see, we're here to discuss adding fruit brandies to the King's Finest Distillery lineup. A venture Dad, Max and Zora have been pushing for some time now." Duke nodded in their general direction. "I think the company and the market are in a good place now for us to explore the possibility."

Max should be riveted by the conversation. After all, this project was one he'd been fighting for the past thirty months. Yet it took every ounce of self-control he could muster to keep from blatantly staring at the beautiful woman seated directly across the table from him.

Peaches. Or rather, Quinn Bazemore. Dixon Bazemore's granddaughter. She was more gorgeous than he remembered. Her beautiful brown skin looked silky and smooth.

The simple, gray shift dress she wore did its best to mask her shape. Still, it was obvious her hips and breasts were fuller now than they'd been the last time he'd held her in his arms. The last time he'd seen every square inch of that shimmering brown skin.

Zora elbowed him again and he held back an audible *oomph*.

"What's with you?" she whispered.

"Nothing," he whispered back.

So maybe he wasn't doing such a good job of masking his fascination with Quinn. He'd have to work on the use of his peripheral vision.

Max opened his booklet to the page his father indicated. He was thrilled that the company was ready to give their brandy initiative a try, even if it was just a test run for now.

It was obvious why Mr. Bazemore was there. His farm could provide the fruit for the brandy. But that didn't explain what on earth Quinn Bazemore—his ex—was doing there.

Don't miss what happens next in
A Reunion of Rivals *by Reese Ryan.*

Available July 2020 wherever
Harlequin Desire books and ebooks are sold.

Harlequin.com

Copyright © 2020 by Roxanne Ravenel

Get 4 FREE REWARDS!

We'll send you 2 FREE Books plus 2 FREE Mystery Gifts.

Harlequin Desire® books transport you to the world of the American elite with juicy plot twists, delicious sensuality and intriguing scandal.

FREE Value Over $20

YES! Please send me 2 FREE Harlequin Desire novels and my 2 FREE gifts (gifts are worth about $10 retail). After receiving them, if I don't wish to receive any more books, I can return the shipping statement marked "cancel." If I don't cancel, I will receive 6 brand-new novels every month and be billed just $4.55 per book in the U.S. or $5.24 per book in Canada. That's a savings of at least 13% off the cover price! It's quite a bargain! Shipping and handling is just 50¢ per book in the U.S. and $1.25 per book in Canada.* I understand that accepting the 2 free books and gifts places me under no obligation to buy anything. I can always return a shipment and cancel at any time. The free books and gifts are mine to keep no matter what I decide.

225/326 HDN GNND

Name (please print)

Address _____ Apt. #

City _____ State/Province _____ Zip/Postal Code

Mail to the Reader Service:
IN U.S.A.: P.O. Box 1341, Buffalo, NY 14240-8531
IN CANADA: P.O. Box 603, Fort Erie, Ontario L2A 5X3

Want to try 2 free books from another series? Call 1-800-873-8635 or visit www.ReaderService.com.

---

*Terms and prices subject to change without notice. Prices do not include sales taxes, which will be charged (if applicable) based on your state or country of residence. Canadian residents will be charged applicable taxes. Offer not valid in Quebec. This offer is limited to one order per household. Books received may not be as shown. Not valid for current subscribers to Harlequin Desire books. All orders subject to approval. Credit or debit balances in a customer's account(s) may be offset by any other outstanding balance owed by or to the customer. Please allow 4 to 6 weeks for delivery. Offer available while quantities last.

Your Privacy—The Reader Service is committed to protecting your privacy. Our Privacy Policy is available online at www.ReaderService.com or upon request from the Reader Service. We make a portion of our mailing list available to reputable third parties that offer products we believe may interest you. If you prefer that we not exchange your name with third parties, or if you wish to clarify or modify your communication preferences, please visit us at www.ReaderService.com/consumerschoice or write to us at Reader Service Preference Service, P.O. Box 9062, Buffalo, NY 14240-9062. Include your complete name and address.

HD20R

**IF YOU ENJOYED THIS BOOK
WE THINK YOU WILL ALSO LOVE**

HARLEQUIN
PRESENTS

Escape to exotic locations where passion knows no bounds.

Welcome to the glamorous lives of royals and billionaires, where passion knows no bounds. Be swept into a world of luxury, wealth and exotic locations.

8 NEW BOOKS AVAILABLE EVERY MONTH!

HPXSERIES2020

Love Harlequin romance?

DISCOVER.

Be the first to find out about promotions,
news and exclusive content!

Facebook.com/HarlequinBooks

Twitter.com/HarlequinBooks

Instagram.com/HarlequinBooks

Pinterest.com/HarlequinBooks

ReaderService.com

EXPLORE.

Sign up for the Harlequin e-newsletter and
download a free book from any series at
TryHarlequin.com

CONNECT.

Join our Harlequin community to
share your thoughts and connect
with other romance readers!
Facebook.com/groups/HarlequinConnection

HSOCIAL2020

Heartfelt or suspenseful, inspiring or passionate, Harlequin has your happily-ever-after.

With new books published every month, you are sure to find the satisfying escape you know you deserve.

SIGN UP FOR THE HARLEQUIN NEWSLETTER

Be the first to hear about great new reads and exciting offers!

Harlequin.com/newsletters

HNEWS2020